GONERS

6/ UNDER LOCH AND KEY

6/ UNDER LOCH AND KEY

JAMIE SIMONS
and E.W. SCOLLON

Illustrations by MICHAEL EVANS

AN AVON CAMELOT BOOK

This is a work of fiction. Names, characters, places, and incidents either are the product of the author's imagination or are used fictitiously. Any resemblance to actual events, locales, organizations, or persons, living or dead, is entirely coincidental and beyond the intent of either the author or the publisher.

AVON BOOKS, INC.
1350 Avenue of the Americas
New York, New York 10019

Copyright © 1998 by Jamie S. Simons and E.W. Scollon, Jr.
Interior illustrations copyright © 1998 by Michael Evans
Interior illustrations by Michael Evans
Published by arrangement with the authors
Visit our website at **http://www.AvonBooks.com**
Library of Congress Catalog Card Number: 98-93053
ISBN: 0-380-79735-6

First Avon Camelot Printing: November 1998

CAMELOT TRADEMARK REG. U.S. PAT. OFF. AND IN OTHER COUNTRIES, MARCA REGISTRADA, HECHO EN U.S.A.

Printed in the U.S.A.

OPM   10 9 8 7 6 5 4 3 2 1

With love to my Grandma Chism,
one of my favorite Earthlings,
on her 90th birthday.

—E.W.S.

To my Grandmother Mae,
who taught me humor and wisdom
are two sides of the same coin.

—J.S.

ACKNOWLEDGMENTS

Special thanks to John Hennessy, Emily Hutta, and Lisa Sturz. Thanks too to Bette Gould for being such a fan.

6/ UNDER LOCH AND KEY

1

Arms Akimbo

A gray blob-of-a-creature was sliding down a hill right toward me! It tumbled end over end, laughing insanely. Then, *splat*, it splashed me from head to toe with bright pink Planetoid Roma mud. *Yecch!*

My hypermemory projector was playing back scenes on the inside of my eyelids like a holographic movie. Next, I saw the creature more clearly—sluglike, with spiked hair and eyes all around his head. Except only two were real. It was hard to tell if he was coming or going. Kind of cute, if you like that sort of thing.

Finally, I saw myself at a Bottom Feeder feast. Watching, amazed as he first chewed up his food, then pulled it from his mouth and smeared it like chunky

1

paste all over his blubbery body, so he could soak up the nutrients. Not so cute.

"I really miss him!" I cried, my eyes flying open.

The others in Dr. Autonomou's lab were stunned. "We all do, Arms," said my best friend Xela. "We'll get him back," added Rubidoux. But you could see he was worried. The purple tentacles on his head, antennae really, were just sitting there, not moving a bit the way they did when he was happy.

"She-Rak will not be abandoned," Gogol said. The four of us were standing in the spot where, moments before, an intergalactic wormhole had suddenly opened, then just as suddenly, slammed shut, taking our classmate and kind of, sort of friend, She-Rak, with it.

"We can't give up on him," I said to Dr. Autonomou and the Grand DOO-DUH. This was Autonomou's secret lab. She was the genius behind the whole operation. And the Grand DOO-DUH was, well . . . he was the big guy, head of Diplomatic Universal Headquarters, where Arms, Xela, Rubi, and I were studying to become interplanetary diplomats. "She-Rak may be a little gross, a little smelly, and kind of a big lug, but he's not a bad guy."

"We have no intention of giving up on him, Arms," Autonomou said. "But it's not going to be easy to get him back. I did not have time to enact the trace program on the computer. I have no way of knowing what planet he transported himself to."

"All right, life forms," Dandoo the Grand DOO-DUH announced. "Let's go over just exactly what happened." He ruffled his multicolored feathers and scrunched up his orange beak. The long black robe made him look very official. Which, I guess, was the point.

2

Dandoo, the Decidedly Officious Official of Diplomatic Universal Headquarters, was one of the most powerful life forms in the whole P.U. And there are 127 worlds of the Planetary Union, including my own home of Armegettem.

"First, She-Rak followed me here," Gogol said meekly.

"You should have been more careful," Autonomou said. "He never would have found the lab, if not for you." She was right, of course. Autonomou's lab was far underground in the deepest, darkest part of Tunnel Thirteen. Xela, Rubi, and I found it only by taking a wrong turn down a dead end and falling through a secret door.

Rubidoux spoke next. "Then, She-Rak grabbed the WAT-Man from me."

"A Warp-Time Manipulator in the hands of an amateur is dangerous," Dandoo said, pacing the floor. "Any mission specialist knows that."

"We're not technically mission specialists yet, Mr. DOO-DUH, sir," I pointed out. "I mean we have several more years of school ahead of us first. Then there's the selection process, special training, the test missions . . ."

"Exactly my point," DOO-DUH said, glaring. "Yet you have assumed the role of mission specialists by going on secret missions to RU1:2. So you must act accordingly."

"Yes, sir."

"Anyway," Rubi continued, "She-Rak grabbed the WAT-Man, and before I could get it back, he was jabbing his finger at it. He must have accidentally entered

3

some weird coordinates because a wormhole opened up.''

"When he saw what he had done, he panicked," Xela said. "Unfortunately, he ran right into the wormhole. Then, whoosh! It closed and he was gone." Xela was one shade beyond concern. Her bright blue skin had lost its color and the light from the prism-like eye in the back of her head was dim. That didn't happen very often.

"And, I'm afraid he may stay gone." Dr. Autonomou sighed as her huge green body plopped into the computer chair, which moaned. Perched at the end of stubby stalks, the doctor's two large eyes roamed over the homemade control panel.

"But there're only about five billion populated worlds out there," Rubi said. "If we start now, we should done by dinner!"

"Rubi, this is serious," Xela said.

"I know, I know," he said. "It's too bad we don't have the WAT-Man."

"Right," Autonomou agreed. "I could transfer the internal files to the main unit, analyze the bits and bobs in the database, and reconstruct the coordinates."

"But She-Rak took it with him, didn't he?" I asked.

"I think so," Rubi said.

"You think so?" Dandoo roared. "Think like a mission specialist! That means there's a chance he left it here, right?"

"I guess . . ."

"Well, then, let's search the lab!" Dandoo commanded. "Look along the walls, under the workbench, behind the piles of junk . . ."

4

"That 'junk', as you call it, is a project I've been working on," Autonomou said.

"My apologies, Doctor." Dandoo smiled. The four of us spread out through Dr. A.'s cave of a lab while Dandoo stood beside her at the computer. I started at the farthest point, the secret door that led to the Tunnels. Nothing there. Then I began working my way across the room, looking in the shadows and behind the odd pieces of equipment lying against the walls. I guess this must have seemed like a good time for a lecture, because Dandoo the Grand-guy launched into a big one.

"I still don't see how this could have happened," he began. "You four students represent the best the Planetary Union has to offer. I pride myself on seeing that here at DUH we take only the most talented life forms in the P.U."

"Thank you! Thank you!" said Rubi to no one in particular as he searched near the wall-sized computer screen.

"The future peace of the Union is in your hands. When you graduate, you will serve as diplomats on one of the Union's 127 member planets. It is the highest honor there is."

Dandoo was right, of course. We'd probably be peace diplomats. *Unless* we were chosen to be mission specialists. That's the really cool job. You get to go to war-torn planets, take the shape of the life forms there, and teach them the ways of peace. Then, if you're successful, and that planet attains full-time peace, it will be invited by the High Council to join the P.U. If not, the planet is left alone. Cut off forever. But it would be years before we found out if we would make it to mission specialist school. Except for Xela. She had already

5

been chosen. That tells you how smart she is. I moved down the wall and started to search near Autonomou's collection of artifacts from planet RU1:2—Earth, as the locals called it.

"Despite all this," the DOO-DUH continued, "you have chosen to violate the High C's eternal ban on travel to RU1:2."

"But Mr. Grand DOO-DUH, sir," Gogol said, crawling out from under the workbench, "one hundred seventy-five mission specialists were abandoned there. Stranded by the High Council because of a terrible mix-up. Once we learned the truth, we couldn't just stand by and do nothing. We had to help Autonomou bring them back."

"And they came just at the right time," Autonomou said. "I had been working two hundred years to re-establish a wormhole link to Earth. Of course, Dandoo, I couldn't have done it without you."

By accident Xela, Gogol, Rubi, and I had learned that the Grand DOO-DUH had been helping Autonomou in secret for the past two hundred years. But if he heard her now, he pretended not to. Instead, he just kept talking . . .

"What you've started here is dangerous," Dandoo said. "I'm scared, Doctor, and not too proud to admit it—"

"I found it!" Xela called from the middle of the room. Her back was toward me, but colored light was streaming from her look-back eye and reflecting off the shelves next to me. "I see the WAT-Man!"

I started rummaging through the stuff on the shelves. "Where?" I shrieked. The shelves were covered with the things Autonomou had sucked up from Earth while

6

she was trying to get the wormhole working again. Pieces of stamped metal called "keys" and "coins," head gear, puzzling pieces, homework and tons of mismatched foot warmers Earthlings called "socks."

"Here it is!" Xela cried as she reached into the pile.

"Brilliant!" said Rubi.

"Excellent!" Gogol agreed.

"Hold on, She-Rak!" I yelled. "Student geniuses to the rescue!"

"Not so fast, Arms," Autonomou said as she took the unit from Xela. "We must focus on the task at hand."

"Which hand would that be?" I asked, holding up all four of mine. "The top left? Top right? Bottom left, or . . ."

"Arms, please."

The mention of hands made mine tingle. I stretched my arms over my head and cracked the knuckles on all twenty-four of my triple-jointed fingers. The crackling filled the lab and sounded like a seven-spined Sky Semptor getting his necks chyro-adjusted.

Autonomou chuckled. "I'm afraid this will not be a quick process. It will take me at least several ikrons to sort all this data out."

"Perfect!" Dandoo chirped.

"Perfect?" asked Gogol.

"Yes, perfect. That will be just long enough for the four of you to get to class. Don't forget, I am still the head of DUH, and it is still my responsibility to see that students attend school. So get going, all of you."

"Oh," I groaned. "I'm so worried about She-Rak. How am I supposed to pay attention in class?"

"That's what a good mission specialist does, Arms,"

Dandoo said. "You must stay sane as senselessness swamps."

Half the time, I didn't have a clue what this guy was talking about, but whatever. He was in charge. I smiled at Autonomou, then followed the others toward the back door and the Alleviator that would take us back up to Roma's surface.

"Promise we can come back as soon as our classes are over?" asked Xela.

"Of course," said Dandoo. "We should have the code by then. And remember, Professor Hal E. Toesis is already suspicious of you four. He's made an appointment to see the High Council. If they find his concerns worthy of investigation, it's a mere matter of time until they pull the plug on this operation. Dr. Autonomou will be exiled, and all of you will be expelled. So if you see him, act dumb."

"No problem," I said.

"That's what I'm afraid of, Arms. That's exactly what I'm afraid of."

2

Rubidoux

The four of us crowded into the Alleviator and pushed the key for ground zero. The Alleviator is one of Autonomou's inventions—she thinks it's a riot that this moving puff of air "alleviates" the need for stairs. Personally, I don't always get her sense of humor. But as we whizzed toward the surface, I was grateful for her smarts. The Tunnels may be a more fun way of getting to and from the lab, but this was a whole lot faster.

Usually. As we got close to the crust bubble—kind of a trap door to the surface—everything stopped. Dead.

"Uh-oh," Arms said.

"Rubi, what's wrong?" asked Xela.

"Beats me," I admitted. "We just stopped for no reason."

"There has to be a reason," Gogol said.

"Eeooww. What's that smell?" Arms asked, clamping two of her hands over her smeller.

"Maybe the Alleviator's retro-resistors burning up?" suggested Xela.

"Brilliant conclusion," I answered with a smirk. "Except this thing doesn't have any."

"There's only one thing on this planet that smells that bad," said Gogol.

"An after-dinner belch from She-Rak," pronounced Arms.

"No," interrupted Xela, "it's the sludge in the ditch that comes from the school cafeteria."

"You're both wrong," I corrected them. "That's the smell from the water in the Roma Gardens fountain where I washed off the slime from planet Mollux."

"Wrong, wrong, and wrong," said Gogol. "Try the sulfur-sucking master of misinformation: DUH's own Professor Hal E. Toesis."

"Of course," said Arms. "I'd recognize that smell anywhere."

"But where's it coming from?" Xela asked.

Gogol pointed straight up. "He must be standing right on top of the crust bubble."

"No wonder we can't get up," I whispered. "We're trapped. How do you think he found us?"

"I'm not so sure he did," said Gogol. "Listen." We all fell quiet, straining our aural sensors. After a moment, I heard it.

"Tal—lu—lah." Toesis was calling Autonomou's

10

first name. "Tallulah! Where are you hiding? It's me, Hal. Come out, Tallulah. I won't harm you."

"Tallulah, again?" I asked. "What's with this guy and the Doc?"

"I don't know, but every time his name comes up, a kind of sadness comes across Autonomou's face," Xela said.

"I say we try to reach through the crust bubble and tickle his toesies," Arms said. "That'll make him move."

"I'm not sure his species even has toes, Arms," I said, hitting the Alleviator key, which sent us flying back down the shaft. "No, what we need to do is talk to Tallulah-baby."

It only took a few moments to be zipped back deep underground. As we made our way from the Alleviator back to the lab, we could hear Autonomou and Dandoo.

"He won't stop until he finds me," Autonomou was saying. "Let's face it, Dandoo. He hates me."

"Hate is a strong word," Dandoo replied. "Especially here on Roma."

"But if he tells the High Council what he knows, it will start a terrible chain of events. You may even lose your job for protecting me," Autonomou raged. "If that's not hate, what is it?"

"It's a life form who has lost everything that was important to him," Dandoo said gently. The four of us stood perfectly still, not even breathing. They were obviously talking about Toesis. Xela was right; there was something big going on.

I heard Autonomou sigh. "I know he'll never forgive me for the loss of his daughter," she groaned. *Whoa!* I turned to look at the others. Three sets of unbelieving eyes stared back at me. Shocked.

"Hal E. Toesis had a daughter?" Arms whispered. I motioned for her to hush. By now, the sound of soft sobs were coming from the lab.

Autonomou sniffled. "But she was my daughter, too." Arms let out a gasp.

"What was that?" Autonomou shouted. Arms instantly covered her mouth with all four hands. But it was too late. I could already hear the Grand DOO-DUH's feathered feet sweeping toward the hall where we stood.

"Hello?" he called. "Who's there?"

The four of us scrambled back to the Alleviator and sprawled out on the floor, trying to make it look as if we had just arrived.

"Whew, that was a tough landing!" I said. Out of the corner of my eye, I saw the Grand DOO-DUH approaching.

"Oh hello, Grand DOO-DUH, sir," Arms said a little too stiffly. "We came back down because we ran into Toesis."

"You what?"

"Well, we didn't exactly run into him," I said. "He was standing on the crust bubble."

"We were trapped," said Xela.

"So we came back down for help," Gogol added.

"Just this moment?" the Grand DOO-DUH asked slyly. We all looked at each other. Telling a lie went against the Planetary Union's Code of Values. And to lie to the Grand DOO-DUH would be unforgivable. So we all just stared at him. No one spoke.

Except Arms. "This moment. The last moment. The next. Time is relative," she said with a shrug.

The DOO-DUH ruffled his feathers. "I take it you heard us talking."

"I'm afraid so," Gogol admitted. "We didn't mean to."

Dandoo sighed and looked sternly at each of us. "Let's just keep this between us, all right? The good doctor doesn't need to know what you heard. Agreed?"

We all nodded.

"Good," Dandoo said. "Now follow me. It's time we took care of the nosy Professor Toesis once and for all."

"Take care of him?" I said.

"Right." Dandoo snorted. "Send him to his resting place."

The four of us looked at each other. I gulped, then coughed. Then shuffled my feet. I couldn't bring myself to look at the DOO-DUH. "I'm sorry, sir," I sputtered out. "We can't help you with this."

"Very well," the officious official replied. "I suppose you're too young to be involved in a nasty business like this."

That did it. I'd always had a lot of respect for the guy, but it left me in that moment. He had gone too far. No matter how bad things were, there was no way I could let him go off and get Professor Toesis. It was wrong, terribly wrong. I lunged and grabbed him by his feathered arm.

"Rubidoux!" he shrieked. "What do you think you're doing?"

"I must report you to the High Council, sir. All this pressure has taken its toll. You're not thinking clearly."

"Just because I want to send Professor Toesis on vacation?"

"Vacation?" I said, loosening my grip. "You said it was going to be nasty business!"

"And it is," replied the DOO-DUH, yanking his arm from my grasp. "Have you ever tried to book a trip in high season? Almost impossible. It will take all of my considerable power to make it happen."

"Sorry," I mumbled. "Guess I misunderstood."

"You think?" Gogol said, never one to pass up taking a shot at me.

"It's all right, Rubi," Dandoo cooed. "You see, Professor Toesis has a little vacation habitat on a distant moon. Nice place. Tangerine seas, marmalade skies. I'm going to arrange for him to go there for a while."

"How long?" asked Gogol. I could see by the look on his face that he was hoping it would be long enough for us to get all the Goners back from Earth. Gogol was part Earthling and part Alzorian, a mutant unlike anyone else in the Planetary Union. And he had no idea why. So he was obsessed both with finding all the Goners and spending as much time on Earth as possible, to try to find the secret of his origin.

"He'll be gone as long as it takes to get She-Rak back," said the DOO-DUH. "But after that, this lab and Autonomou's missions to find the Goners must cease and desist. Forever!"

3

Xela Zim Bareen

We followed Dandoo back down the hall to Autonomou's lab. I was feeling really weird about the conversation we'd overheard. Dr. Tallulah Autonomou and Professor Hal E. Toesis had once been—gulp—husband and wife. I couldn't see it. But Dandoo had made clear it was true from the way he acted. Now we had to face Autonomou and pretend we hadn't heard a thing. My heart was racing. I'm not too good at keeping secrets.

"What was that noise?" Autonomou asked Dandoo as we came through the door. Then she noticed us. "And why aren't the four of you in class as instructed?"

"They couldn't get through the crust bubble, doctor.

15

Seems a certain Professor Toesis is standing on it," Dandoo said.

"Oh, dear. He's returned to the spot where I let him catch a glimpse of me," Autonomou moaned.

"You let him see you?" Dandoo exclaimed.

"She did it to distract him from seeing us," explained Rubi.

"Oohh, don't tell me any more, please," Dandoo the DOO-DUH begged. The multicolored feathers on his face were quivering. "I've had about all I can take. Being the Grand DOO-DUH is basically a nice, easy desk job. I'm not used to all this danger and suspense."

Arms ran up and gave him a four-arm full-press hug. "Those days are behind you, Grand DOO-DUH, sir. You're one of us. Life will be much more fun now!"

"Thank you, Arms. I think." At least his orange beak was turned up in a smile. And his feathers had settled down again. "Now Doctor, if you'll excuse me. I need a quiet place to communicate with my office."

"Of course, but why?"

"I'm sending Toesis on a forced R and R."

"By the six stars of Erin, no!" Autonomou shouted as she shot up out of her chair. "He may be causing us trouble, but he hardly deserves to be Reset and Reprogrammed!"

"Calm down, Doctor! I'm talking about Rest and Relaxation."

"Oh, of course," Autonomou said.

"An escort will pick him up in Roma Gardens Park, and he'll be gone in less than an ikron."

"Very good idea, Dandoo. Thank you," said Autonomou.

"Don't mention it. I'll just step back into the Alleviator room for a moment and make the arrangements."

"Right," Autonomou said as Dandoo left the room.

"So, Doctor, has the computer figured out where She-Rak went yet?" asked Gogol.

"Not exactly, but it has narrowed down the choices to three," Autonomou said, reading data off the wall-sized computer screen.

"That's not too bad," Arms offered. "You could send one of us to each place and still have someone here to help with the controls."

"Hmmm . . . I suppose I could do that," Autonomou said. "But who would go where? That could be a tough decision."

"Why?" I asked.

"Well, look at the choices." Autonomou directed our attention to the coordinates on the screen. "Planet 2HOT4-U for instance. Covered entirely in constantly shifting tidal waves of sand. Populated by carnivorous sand snakes."

"Snakes?" Gogol shuddered. "Why does it have to be snakes?"

"Surface temperature, searing. The only way She-Rak could have survived is if he burrowed into the sand. And if he did that, I'm afraid he's a sand snake snack by now."

"That's awful," Arms said. "I mean, I know I used to complain about the way She-Rak walked around with clumps of half-digested food hanging off him. But now that I think about it, it was kind of, sort of cute."

"What's the next possible planet, Doctor?" I asked.

"Planet K-OSS," Autonomou said.

"Is it hot there too?"

17

"No, actually, Xela, the weather is quite comfortable. However, finding She-Rak would be impossible."

"I hate to remind you, Doctor," Rubidoux said. "But we've gotten pretty good at finding life forms on alien worlds."

"That's true, Rubi," Autonomou agreed. "But every speck of planet K-OSS is covered by swarming life forms. They are packed in so tightly that when one moves, they all move. The entire planet is covered with creatures who are in constant motion, kept alive by nutrients that rain from the sky."

"Their food falls like rain?" I gasped.

"Of course," the doctor answered. "That's why they have those huge mouths on top of their heads. They just open them up whenever it rains and help themselves to dinner."

"Ugh, sounds like an awful life." Arms sighed.

"They like it. But I'm afraid if She-Rak landed in the middle of that crowd, he'd be swept up instantly. There's no way you'd find him."

"But there is one more possibility, right?" Rubi said.

"Correct. It's coming up on screen now. There," she said, pointing to the coordinates on the giant display. "Planet RU1:2."

"Earth!"

Gogol perked up when the coordinates for Earth came on screen. "So which planet is the most likely one, Doctor?"

Autonomou smiled, reached under the computer console, and pulled out a heavy and strange-looking machine. "This thing came flying out of the wormhole about fifty years ago, and I've been waiting for a chance to use it. Arms, hand me some coins from the artifact shelf.''

"What is it?" I asked, looking it over. It had three little windows with pictures of Earth-type fruit in them, an open tray at the bottom, and one long handle attached to the side.

"I believe it's an Earthling odds calculator," Autonomou said. "Simply ask it a question, drop in a coin, and pull the handle. Then you interpret the symbols in the three little windows to get the answer. Ready?"

"I guess," Arms said. We all nodded.

"Then here we go. First planet, 2H-OT4-U!" She dropped in a coin and pulled the handle. The pictures in the window spun around, then came to a stop, one at a time. "Lemon, orange, cherry. Aha! Nothing matches. There is no chance She-Rak is there."

"That's an amazing machine, Doctor," I said.

"Isn't it? Now let's try planet K-OSS." Again the pictures flew through the window and clicked to a stop. "Lemon, cherry, lemon! The odds for K-OSS are much better."

"Please be Earth, please be Earth," we all began to chant.

"Is it RU1:2?" Autonomou asked the machine. She gave the handle a mighty pull. We all watched the fruit windows. "Cherry, cherry . . . cherry!"

"We have a winner!" the machine announced. Bells rang, lights flashed, and tons of those little round coins came pouring out of the tray at the bottom.

"It can't be much clearer than that!" Autonomou said. "She-Rak is definitely on Earth."

"Wow," Arms said, "Of all the places he could have ended up! That's quite a coinky-dinky, isn't it?"

19

"It would seem so. But I suspect that when She-Rak was poking at the WAT-Man, he entered a sequence that successfully opened a wormhole, but that didn't have a valid set of coordinates. So the computer assigned the last destination that was entered."

"Looks like we're going back to Paris, 1888, Xela!" Rubi laughed. "Makes sense to send us, Doctor, since we know our way around. And, I know all about ordering hot chocolate and fries."

"I wish it was that easy, my friends. She-Rak managed to change the code just enough so that he landed in a different time and place. But at least we know he's on Earth. The computer will retrace the energy pathway that was created by the wormhole and drop you off where it dropped him. But where that is and when will be a mystery until you get there."

"So what are we waiting for?" Rubi said. "Send me in, Coach!"

"Rubi," Gogol said seriously. "Have you forgotten what the grand DOO-DUH said?"

"Everybody in the pool?"

"No, Rubi, I'm serious," Gogol said. "He said this would absolutely, positively be the last mission, remember?"

"Yeah, I guess I remember that," Rubi answered. We were quiet while the thought sunk in. It was sad. We had all come to like Earth: its one pale yellow sun, the flavored Fizz of Life, the tubular cream-filled sponge cakes, and the funny way humans all looked alike, but thought they were so different. Now that would be behind us. After this mission, it would be over.

"Listen, guys," Gogol said. He looked tense. I knew what was coming. If he was ever going to find out why he looked like an Earthling in spite of being from a planet of reptile-like life forms, this was the time. I felt sorry for him. "I know how much each of us wants to go to Earth one last time, but I'm asking you, pleading with you really, to send me."

"Didn't really want to see the old place anyway," squeaked Arms. I knew she didn't mean it, and technically I guess you could say she was going against the Code of Values by not saying how she really felt. But looking at the smile on Gogol's face, I have to say I was proud of her.

"Okay," said Rubi. "If two of us go, as usual, then that leaves either Xela or me." Then he shot me a Rubi, one of his trademark dazzling smiles. I consider Rubi my very best friend, and I'm a sucker for that look. "Have a heart, Xela. This will be my last chance to try to find that lovely creature I met on my first trip."

"Are you talking about Rebecca or that kid you called Red-with-an-attitude?" Gogol laughed.

"Rebecca, of course. She told me to 'give her a call.' This will be my last chance to find out what a 'call' is, and actually give it to her. Come on Xela, tell me you won't stand in the way of true love."

"Rubi, I think I can actually hear your four hearts pounding from across the room. If it's that important to you, you go."

"Thanks," Rubi said, giving me an Earthling hug. He knew that would seal the deal. I can't resist a hug.

"Dr. Autonomou," I called out, "we're ready."

Autonomou turned her left eye stalk to me. "Good, I'm nearly ready as well. This old computer is giving me a little trouble, but I think the program will stick.

Now let's get you all to Earth before this old system blows a fuse."

"All of us?" I said. "But, Doctor, you told us before that only two could go on a mission."

"This is an exception," Autonomou said. "From what you've told me about Earthlings, they're not going to know what to do with a Bottom Feeder like She-Rak. And that frightens me. You must find him as quickly as possible. So I'm sorry, but you all need to go."

"Roma-rama!" yelled Arms as we all gathered in the middle of the room. "Rubi, grab a couple extra pan-tawkies!"

"Four pan-tawkies present and accounted for!" Rubi said, handing out the tiny language translators that made it possible to communicate with species outside the P.U.

"I've entered the coordinates from the screen into the WAT-Man, Doctor," Gogol said.

"Excellent," Autonomou called. "You'll be on your way momentarily!"

"Coordinates for Planet RU1:2 confirmed," the computer announced cheerfully. "Stand-by for warp-time travel."

The four of us joined hands as the air in the lab began to vibrate. Invisible waves began to ripple through the air as ice cold wind swirled around us and an intergalactic highway opened up.

"Wormhole materializing!" the computer chirped.

"Wait! Hold everything!" Arms shouted.

"It's too late to stop!" Autonomou screamed. "What's wrong?"

"Group hug!" Arms squealed over the roar of the wormhole. She put all four arms out as wide as they could go. We all squished together and took a step forward.

"Good luck," Dr. Autonomou called.

"Safe travel," said Dandoo.

"Toodles," Arms said, as the four of us dematerialized and vanished into the wormhole.

4

Arms Akimbo

Our group hug turned into a group tumble as the wormhole spit us out on the side of a steep hill. "Don't let go!" I squealed, using all four of my own arms and twenty-four triple-jointed fingers to keep everyone in a firmly held ball. "Yee-hah!"

"Ooooh," "Ow," and "Ugh" were all I heard back from the others. Finally we hit level ground and sprawled out in the rough green stubble.

"That was fun!" I said, staring into the blue Earth sky and trying to catch my breath. No matter how many times I've come here, Earth always surprises me. On the one hand, it's completely different from Roma. On the other hand, it's a lot the same. Different and the same at the same time, if you see what I mean. Different: Earth has a blue sky. Roma's is orange. Different: Earth has one sun. Roma has two. Different: Earth has a lot of green and brown. Roma is more colorful. Like on Roma, mud is pink and plant life is mostly shades of purple.

So what's the same? Same: Breathable air—although Earth doesn't really have a healthy level of ozone—but it's enough to keep alien life forms alive. Same: Gravity. Earth has a very friendly supply. Not too much. Not too little. It's just right. Same: Many life forms. Earth has tons of them. But humans seem to think they're the only intelligent beings on the planet. Wrong. Unfortunately, they are the only life form we can communicate with. Only human languages are entered into our pantawky translators. Autonomou says she's working on loading in dog, horse, bird, mosquito, butterfly, and a few other important Earthling species, but it hasn't happened yet. Too bad. After what Xela told me about coming to Earth and living as a dog, I get the feeling humans may be the *least* intelligent life forms on this planet.

"Come on," Gogol said with a little edge in his voice. We can't just lie around here all day."

"Okay, fine," I said, handspringing into a standing position. "So where's She-Rak?"

"Must have wandered off," Rubi said, looking in every direction. The purple tentacles on his head were in full squirm mode. "I'm scanning for life forms, but not picking up any intelligent life."

"Gee, thanks," I teased.

Rubidoux smiled. "With the exception of you, Arms."

I stood up on a rock and looked around. We were at the side of a long, skinny body of dark water, surrounded by steep, rocky hills. I could see pretty far because there weren't too many big trees. But no luck. I didn't see any baggy creatures like She-Rak. "I bet he went somewhere to find food. He said he was hungry."

"Oooh," said Rubi. "Think he might have gone in search of the Fizz of Life?"

"Not She-Rak's style," I reminded Rubi. "He wouldn't go near suspended CO_2 flavored with cola. Or the cream-filled sponge cakes Gogol loves. Or . . ."

"Will you two cut it out?" barked Xela. "What is it with everyone and Earthling food?"

"You said yourself the cakes were pretty good at Monticello," I reminded her.

"But She-Rak is a Bottom Feeder!" wailed Xela.

"That's true," I said. "Hey, Gogol, too bad we didn't have him with us when we went to London. He would have loved all the slop they threw in the streets. Bottom Feeder heaven!" That's when Xela grabbed me.

"Arms," she said. "Look directly into my two front eyes."

"Okay," I said, staring into her yellow pupils. "The coordinates indicated She-Rak would be somewhere near here."

"Wherever *here* is," Rubi chimed in.

"Don't you start," Xela called to him without once taking her eyes off mine. "Now focus. Everyone focus. Where would She-Rak go to try to find food?"

"Got me," Rubi answered.

"It's got to smell pungent, stinky, and rotten," said Gogol.

We all sniffed the air. Xela tipped her head down to

26

fully open the breathing ports in her neck. Rubi turned his face into the breeze. His species has kind of a nose, but they don't draw air in. It just kind of wafts in on its own. I used my sniffer, sampling the air in short bursts. But Gogol is the one we all watched. His Earthling-type nose is by far the best at picking up smells.

"Nothing," he said. "Smells clean and fresh here, that's about it."

"Actually we've got a bigger problem right now than finding She-Rak," warned Xela.

"We do?" I asked.

"I don't see humans to pattern ourselves after," she said. "And if we don't B.O. soon . . ."

"Our DN-Aydoh will harden and we'll spend our time on Earth looking like we do now. Aliens," groaned Rubi. "Just like old times, Xela."

Rubi and Xela weren't able to B.O. on their last mission, but it wasn't their fault. Something went wrong. See, after you step out of a wormhole, the molecules that flew apart while you were traveling stick themselves back together. But it takes some time for them to firm up. And while they're still soft, you can change the way you look. That is, if you know how to do Biological Osmosis, or B.O., which we do, even though it's supposed to be a huge secret.

Actually, it's simple. You just pick a life form to model yourself after, then concentrate. Your DN-Aydoh, the moldable stuff at the core of your being, will change the way you look. And presto, gizorto, you've got the ultimate disguise!

"Nothing is more important to me right now than B.O.," Xela said.

Gogol pointed to a group of woolly four-legged crea-

27

tures munching on grass behind a low rock wall. "How about them?"

"I know what those are," Xela said. "Met some on my last trip. They're baa-baa creatures. My friend P-Air called them 'sheep.' "

"Great! So B.O. into sheep!" said Gogol.

"Easy for you to say, Gogol. You already look so much like an Earthling you don't have to worry about B.O.-ing. But we do. And all I've ever seen sheep do is follow each other around."

"Not to mention that sheep language is not in our pan-tawkies," added Rubi.

"Oh, my," I said, as I suddenly remembered something that made me feel a little woozy. "In England, the king served me kidney pie." I swallowed hard. "Made from sheep kidneys."

"EEOouuww," the others said together.

"Did you eat it?" Rubi asked.

"Of course not," I said. "But I didn't come on this mission to be served up in a pie. Come on, we have to find a human specimen."

"Over here!" Gogol hissed in a loud whisper. "Look!" We all tiptoed over and joined him behind a big bushy Earth plant. Gogol was pointing out into the water.

"A human!" I squealed. An Earth boy was floating in a small kind of floaty thing like I'd seen on Columbus's ship. A "dinghy," I think they'd called it.

"Good, that's a start," Xela said. "Now we need a few other choices. We can't all pattern ourselves after just one Earthling."

"Well, technically, we can," Rubi pointed out. "And we're running out of time."

"LOOK!" Gogol shouted. "What's happening?" We all looked out at the boy. The water around his little dinghy thingy started to churn and heave. The boy was holding on to the sides of his boat and looking down into the water.

Gogol stepped out of the bushes. "Are you okay?" he yelled. Instantly, the water went calm.

"Fine. Fine," called the boy as he picked up two oars and stuck them in the water. "Just a school of fish."

"Must be recess," said Rubi.

5

Gogol

"Gogol!" Xela whispered from the bushes. "Keep that Earthling busy until we're done with our B.O."

"Right," I answered, turning back to the boy moving toward me. "And listen, you guys, I'm no expert on Biological Osmosis, but make sure you finish the change in your mind's eye. Make at least one detail different. If you don't, you'll all look exactly like this specimen."

I turned back around just as the specimen hopped out of his floater and pulled it ashore. "Are you sure that was a school of fish making those huge waves?"

"Aye," he answered.

"You?" I asked.

"Aye," he confirmed.

I was sure I had it wrong, so I began again. Pointing at my eye, I said, "Eye!"

"Aye," he echoed.

"Good," I sighed. "So it wasn't you making those waves." At this the boy cocked his head and began to walk in a wide circle around me. "I don't think I've ever seen you around the loch before."

"Lock?" I held my hands up. "Nope. I'm lockless."

"Loch Less? Is that where you're from? Never heard of it. This is Loch Ness. Most famous lake in Scotland. I don't recognize your clothes. Are you English?"

"No," I answered. "I've been told I'm Russian. So let me quickly get to the point. Have you seen a short, gray, baggy creature that looks like a tadpole with spiked hair?"

"Aha," said the boy. "I might have known. You've heard the rumors of the Loch Ness monster and you've come to see her for yourself." Was She-Rak a monster? I guess he could have looked like one to an Earthling.

"That's right," I said.

"I'll save you time," the boy said. "There's no such thing."

"But the churning water," I pointed out.

"Fish, I told you."

"No unusual slime trails?"

"No," answered the boy.

"No strange raspy-wheezy-burpy sounds?" The boy started to laugh and shake his head from side to side. "Anything unusual at all?" I begged. I felt sure he knew something.

"Well, yes, I have seen some unusual things," he said. *Aha! I knew it!* "There's the likes of you, dressed

31

oddly and asking strange questions. And then there's that bush shaking over there."

I looked over my shoulder. He was right.

"Is someone hiding back there?"

"Hiding?" I said. "No, no. Why would anyone be hiding? No, they're . . . resting." I called out to the bush. "Come on out, everyone." The boy and I watched as a life form came out and stood in front of us.

The boy gasped. "By the Stone of Scone! You could be my twin!"

"Except for the skirt," the B.O. version of the boy said. "See? Your design is right angles. Mine's all kind of tied and dyed." *Oh great,* I thought. The whole point of completing Biological Osmosis in your head is so that you can make changes in your face, not your clothing! Then, the next life form came out from behind the bush and things went from bad to worse.

"Och, aye! He looks the same, too!" the boy exclaimed.

"Not exactly," I sputtered. "Note the skirt. Striped." When my final transformed friend came out, my heart sank—more bad B.O.

"What kind of witchcraft is this!" the boy shouted. "Three lads who look identical to me?"

"Except for the skirt," I reminded him.

"Kilt!" he cried. *Just because their B.O. is bad, you don't have to threaten violence,* I thought. Then he began to make a slow circle around my friends. "I've never seen tartans like these!"

"They're my, um, cousins," I said trying to calm him down. They looked so much alike, I couldn't even tell who was who.

"Is that so? Really?" he said, walking over to examine the identical triplets closely. "What are your names?"

The first one spoke. "I'm Hamish!" he said.

"Why, that's my brother's name!" the boy choked. He looked at the second life form. "And I suppose your name is Hamish, too."

"Nope," came the answer. "Cornish."

"And you?" the boy asked the one in the polka-dot skirt.

"My name? Um . . . Kind-of-ish!" That solved one mystery. At least now I knew which one was Arms.

6

Rubidoux

The Earth boy stood there staring at me, Arms, and Xela, with a look of deep shock. Okay, I admit it. We messed up. We'd forgotten one of the first rules of B.O. Complete the change in your imagination. Otherwise, trouble. Like now. Arms, Xela, and yours truly, all looking almost exactly like the boy. Same height. Same weight. Same face. But at least we *did* pick different patterns for our skirts. And different names. I'd checked into the boy's thoughts and picked a name stuck in his mind: Hamish. That was me. Xela was Cornish, Arms, Kind-of-ish, and the boy's name was . . .

"I'm Jackie," he said.

"Do you live here?" I asked.

"Here? By the side of the loch? No. I live nearby in a town named Farr. And where are you from?"

"Farther," Arms replied.

"Never heard of it," Jackie said. "But it must be awfully far away." Then he pointed at his own skirt. "Your tartans are not from any clans I know."

"Clans?" asked Arms. "Did you say clans?"

"Aye, you know," shrugged Jackie. "Like Ross, Chisholm, Stewart, MacBain, Campbell. There's more than a hundred clans spread through the Highlands. And all their tartans are more or less like mine."

"Would you excuse us for a moment?" Arms asked as she gathered Xela, Gogol, and me into a huddle. "What a break! She-Rak's home planet is divided into clans, remember?"

"That's right," said Xela. "He's part of the Rak clan."

"Yeah, but I don't remember ever seeing him wearing a skirt," I pointed out.

"Of course not, Rubi," Gogol, mister know-it-all, had to say. He never seems to know when I'm kidding.

"Umm . . . Jackie," Arms said as she broke from the huddle. "Have you ever heard of the Rak clan?"

"Rak?" the boy said thoughtfully. "No, I'm afraid I've never heard of them."

"Rats-o-rama," Arms sighed. "Okay then, could you tell us where we'd find rotting, stinking, putrid food."

"That would be the dump. But what would you be wanting with that place?"

"Looking for a friend of ours," I explained.

"Really, now?" said Jackie. "Interesting friend."

"If you'd be so kind as to point the way," said Xela.

"I can do better than that," Jackie said, grabbing a small pack from the floater. "I'm going past there now. I'll take you."

"Are you sure it's not too much trouble?" asked the ever-polite Xela.

"Och, no," answered Jackie. "I haven't been this entertained . . . I mean, it's no trouble at all. Follow me."

"Great," I said. "Let's go!"

"Wait," said Gogol. "Two of us should go and two should stay here in case She-Rak comes back."

"Yeah? And who made you mission control? I think we should stick together." I didn't mean to complain, but Gogol is just a little too bossy for my taste sometimes.

"I don't know, Rubi," Arms said. "I think Gogol's right. Someone should wait here. Look, Xela and I will check out the dump and come right back."

"Aye, aye, Captain," I said, a little annoyed.

"Hey, would you rather go to the dump?" asked Arms.

"No, no. I'm sure Gogol and I will find something to talk about. You and Xela go off and have all the adventure."

"Look, Rubi, you can go if you want," Xela offered. "I mean, we're just going to poke around a bunch of rotten old garbage, so I don't feel like I'll be missing much."

Actually, when she put it like that, staying put sounded pretty good. "No, no. Go ahead," I muttered.

"Aye, you certainly argue like cousins," said Jackie. "Anyone coming with me or not?"

36

"Sure," said Arms, as she and Xela headed off after Jackie.

"Bye!" I called. "Have fun! We'll be right here. Doing nothing. Waiting. Counting sheep."

7

Gogol

Okay, I admit it. I had my own reasons for coming to Earth, and none of them had anything to do with She-Rak. I mean, sure, I wanted to find him and bring him back, but I had another, even more important mission. As I watched the girls and Jackie disappear down the road, the question became, "How am I going to get where I need to go?" Namely, Russia.

Up until my last trip to RU1:2, the only thing I knew for sure was that Earthlings had somehow managed to hop the fence and jump into the deep end of my gene pool. Then on my last trip to Earth—England, 1550s— a wicked duke named Northumberland let it slip that my name, Gogol, was Russian. That was the biggest clue I'd picked up yet about who I might be and why, except for the Alzorian stripe running down my back, I look like an Earthling.

I knew the others must be sick of hearing about how I was like no one else in the Planetary Union. But for me, this was everything. I *had* to discover why I looked like no one else on my planet, not even my parents. And I had no time to waste. The Grand DOO-DUH made it clear that this would be our last mission to Earth. I had to hurry.

"I'm rushin' to Russia, Rubi," I announced. "You're on your own."

"Not so fast," he said. "We just told the girls we'd wait by the lake. You can't leave."

"I can. I must. And I am," I said grandly. "But I shall return!"

"Oh, gee. Okay General, Captain, Admiral, sir," Rubi scoffed. "Who appointed you Grand DOO-DUH? You have to stay here with me. That was the deal."

He was right. That was the deal. But at the risk of making Rubi mad, I had to go. "Rubi, this might be my last—my only—chance to find out who I am. I'm sorry. I have to pay a quick visit to Russia, whether you approve or not."

I took a step, but Rubidoux moved in front of me, blocking my way. "Then I'm going with you," he said, glaring. "We're going to stick together. You know you'll need me. Every time you go anywhere by yourself you make a mess of things."

"What are you talking about?" I shouted. "I'm the one who's always in control!"

"Yeah?" jeered Rubidoux. "Who jumped into a wormhole headed for who-knew-where and got dumped out in a place called Portland at the end of Earth's twentieth century, without a clue how to get home? Who fell through a crust bubble in the Tunnels at P-force speed? Who got locked up in the Tower of London? Who did Thomas Jefferson almost hang as a British spy? You. You. You, you, and you,'' Rubidoux shouted, jabbing at me with his finger. ''I rest my case.''

''Okay,'' I said. ''So I've had a few mishaps. That's all the more reason why you should stay here. I don't want you to stick your neck out for me anymore.'' Then I turned and started to follow a path that seemed to lead to the top of the closest hill. Rubidoux stayed behind.

''Fine,'' Rubidoux yelled after me. ''If that's how you feel, I'll wait here. But do you have any idea where that Russia place is?''

''Not exactly, but I figure if I see a bunch of people rushing around, I must be close, right?'' I called out.

''Huh?''

''I'm going to hop on a high-speed transport of some kind,'' I said. At least, I hoped I would.

''I doubt it, brain-boy,'' Rubi said. ''Seems to me we've landed in a primitive time period again. And if that's true, nothing here moves at high speed.''

''Then I guess I'll walk,'' I shot back. ''All I know is, I have to try.''

''All right,'' called Rubi, ''but I'm warning you. If we're ready to go back to Roma and you're not here, we're going to have to leave without you.''

''That's fine with me,'' I snarled back. ''Just add me to the list of Goners.''

8

Arms Akimbo

It was a pretty long walk. Pretty because yellow light from Earth's sun twinkled on the lake and danced in the trees. Long because Jackie's "couple of miles" was sort of, mainly mostly uphill. We talked. Jackie sang. His favorite song was kind of sad. About a pig named "Old Lang Swine" who'd been forgotten.

I tried to cheer him up by teaching him my favorite Earth song. "TUTTI-FRUTTI-O-RUTTI, TUTTI-FRUTTI-O-RUTTI!" I bellowed at the top of my lungs.

"What language is that?" asked Jackie.

"Yours," I assured him. "Now for the chorus! WHOMP-BAM-BALOO-BA A WHOMP-BAM-BOOM!"

We walked on together, laughing and singing until we came to a place where two roads crossed. "The town dump is just up the road a bit," said Jackie pointing to a hill. "You take the high road."

Xela looked at him. "You're not coming with us?"

"No, I'll take the low road."

"But, we may never meet again!" said Xela.

"Tell you what," said Jackie. "Meet me by the loch tomorrow morning and we'll go for a row."

"Will that work?" I asked surprised. "I mean there's only three of us. To make a really good row, wouldn't you need quite a few life forms standing all nice and straight . . ."

While I talked, Xela grabbed my arm and started dragging me up the high road. "Bye." She waved to Jackie.

"Tomorrow," he said. "Till then may the sun light your path and the wind be at your back."

"And may the First Sun show you the way and the Great Sun sweep up the mess," I added.

Jackie scrunched up his face. "First Sun and Great Sun?"

"It's poetry," said Xela.

"Aye," said Jackie. "You put Robert Burns to shame, Cavendish."

"Thank you," I called, giving him a thumbs up. Then I turned to Xela. "Any idea what he was talking about?"

"Not the slightest," said Xela as we walked along. "But he sure was nice."

"And peaceful," I added. "Makes you wonder why the High Council was so afraid of Earth. I mean, just look at this place. Flowers. Sheep-guys. A blue sky I've

42

learned to like as much as the orange one on Roma. Sweet, delicious smells." I took a deep whiff through my Earthling-type nose. And gagged.

"I take that back. Maybe the High C had the right idea. This place stinks!" I said as I pushed away the tiny life forms buzzing around my head.

Xela pointed up at the mounded piles of yucko. "Looks like we've found the dump. She-Rak! She-R-A-K!"

He was probably too busy stuffing his face to answer. When I looked around, I could see why. There was garbage everywhere. Stinky, disgusting, smelly old garbage. My heart soared. She-Rak would love this place! He had to be here somewhere.

"Come on," said Xela.

"Excuse me?" I answered.

"We need to go look for him."

"Tell you what," I said. "I'll wait here and call for him, okay? She-Rak! She-Rak! Where are you?" Xela had already headed off into the field of disgusting stuff.

"Don't make me do this alone, Arms."

"Fine, fine, fine. But I better not get anything on my shoes," I said as I walked between piles of putrid rot. "Eek!" I screamed.

"What is it?" cried Xela.

"One of your friends."

"One of *my* friends?" Xela asked.

"Rats, Xela. Like the ones you made friends with on Columbus's ship."

"Oh, yeah. There are some over here, too. Hi, guys. How's it going?" They must not have heard her, or else they were too busy burrowing into the mounds of icky-ooky, because they barely looked up.

43

We kept picking our way through the piles, calling for She-Rak and looking in every nook and cranny in case he had fallen asleep all fat and happy.

"Ugh!" Xela grunted. "I wish I could shut off these human smelling ports."

"I know what you mean. But look, Xela, we've tramped through the whole place. If She-Rak's here, he's not telling us."

"Probably doesn't want to share his spoils," said Xela.

"Who can blame him?" I said, laughing. Then I made my way up a small rise, hoping to get a better view.

"Fore!" cried out a voice in the distance. I turned around and looked across a pretty green field, but I couldn't see where the voice was coming from.

"Five!" Xela called back, in an attempt to be friendly. There was no answer. Instead, a small white rock arced through the air, headed right for us.

"Look out, Xela!" I screamed as I threw myself in front of her.

9

Arms Akimbo

"Ow!" I cried as the hard, round rock-thing bounced off my head. I watched as it rolled through the grass and dropped into a small hole.

"Arms, you saved me from getting clobbered," Xela gushed. "Thank you."

"It was nothing," I said, rubbing the bump on my head. "Xela, did you notice anything strange about the hole that thing rolled into?"

"You mean other than the fact that it's perfectly round and has a flag coming out of it?"

"You got it," I said, getting down on all sixes— oops, I mean, all fours—for a closer look. "This is no ordinary hole. I think it's an entrance to a tunnel."

"Arms, look," Xela said, pointing around. "There are other flags just like this one scattered all over. What are they for?"

Xela's really smart, but sometimes she just doesn't show much common sense.

"Isn't it obvious?" I said. "We've just stumbled on evidence of another form of Earthling. Probably little teensy-weensy creatures that live underground."

"Huh?"

"Sure. These flags mark their kingdoms and the little holes are entrances to their underground cities."

"I don't know, Arms. This flag has the number ten on it."

"Right." I love the moments when I'm being brilliant. "It's probably what Earthlings call their address. And someone is bombing their home." I reached down into the hole and plucked out the hard, nasty sphere.

"Arms, you may be right," Xela said, alarmed. "And it looks like the attackers are headed this way!"

I stood up to get a better look. Two large human beings were marching across the field right toward us. One was dressed all in black. One was wearing a skirt. I couldn't believe what I saw. "Boy, Rubi's right. Humans really do have knobby knees."

"Arms! Forget their knobby knees. Look at the clubs they're carrying!"

Good point. Each one was carrying a long, skinny club with a heavy rounded end. And there were even more clubs in bags strapped to their backs.

"Why in Zedoria would they need all those clubs?"

"I guess they get into a lot of fights," Xela said, sounding a little nervous. "After all, this *is* one of the universe's most violent planets."

"Don't worry, Xela. I know just what to do. I'll make a peace offering."

"Good thinking," said Xela. We both took a couple of steps toward the oncoming clubbers. I held the hard white ball out to them.

"Did you lose something?" I called out.

The men came right up to us and stopped. The taller one looked at the ball in my hand, then at me. "You've committed a foul, laddie."

"I think it's you that committed the foul, Knobby, if you don't mind my saying. You're the one that hurled this bomb. If I hadn't pulled it out of the hole, it would have blocked the entrance, trapped the tiny life forms in their homes, cut off their supplies, and caused starvation and certain death."

The two men must have known they'd been caught in the act. They just stood there gaping at me.

"Tiny life forms?" the smaller one repeated. Like he didn't know what I was talking about!

"Playing dumb won't work with me," I said firmly. "I'm on to you. Imagine grown men hurting such tiny beings."

That bent old Knobby in two with laughter. "It's no laughing matter," I scolded.

"You have a great sense of humor, you do," Knobby-knees said. "Tiny beings living underground, indeed. If it's fairies you're looking for, try Fairy Hill over in town!"

All this time, the shorter, darkly dressed man was looking at me very closely. "Just a moment," he said. "You did say you pulled the ball out of the hole, didn't you?"

"Yes, and I hope you're ashamed of yourself."

"Ashamed? I'm proud as punch!"

My heart sank. "There's no hope for this planet, Xela," I muttered.

"A hole in one!" the Punch Guy shouted. "And, Robert, you said a doctor couldn't play golf."

"I have to hand it to you, Dr. Lister. You've proved me wrong."

"You're playing a game?" Xela asked.

"Of course," said Knobby. "What true Highlander hasn't heard of golf? A proud Scottish tradition." Then he slapped me on the back. "Just givin' the old Englishman a run for his money."

"Another proud Scottish tradition," said Lister with a smile.

"Och," said Knobby, turning to me. "And you've been doing a good job of it too. Now how do the folks call you?"

"Loudly," I said.

"He's Kind-of-ish and I'm Cornish," Xela said.

"Identical twins, are you?" asked Knobby.

"Well, actually—" I started.

"Yes," interrupted Xela.

"Well, I be Robert Campbell," said Knobby, "and this is my friend, Joseph Lister, chief surgeon at Glasgow hospital."

"I'm here on vacation. Robert owns the inn where I'm staying."

"And what about you two?" Campbell asked. "First time in Inverness?"

"Oh, yes," Xela said. "Definitely."

"We're looking for someone actually," I said. "Someone who belongs to the Rak clan."

"Say no more," Lister said, holding up his hand.

48

"You must join us for supper. Robert knows all there is to know about clans."

"Yes, you must," urged the Robert guy.

"What do you think, Arms? I mean, Kind-of-ish?" Xela asked.

"Works for me! I'm starved!" I thought they'd be happy, but right away both men started to pull clubs out of their packs. "Hey, take it easy!" I shouted. "We said we'd come!"

"Easy wee one," said Campbell. "We're just going to tee off."

"We have a few more holes to play," Lister explained.

"You can be our caddies, if you like," Campbell said. The nerve of the man. Did he think we'd be honored?

"No thanks," I answered. "I'm a little rusty on my meows."

10

Gogol

I didn't really think Rubi would head back to Roma without me, but with him you could never really tell. At least I knew that Xela would insist that they wait for me. Xela was cool. She seemed to understand me better than anyone else. Arms and Rubi were a little too interested in themselves sometimes, in my opinion. Don't get me wrong; I like them a lot. They can be a lot of fun. The thing is, life isn't always fun and games.

As I started to wander away from the lake, I had to admit I really had no idea how to get to Russia. But I knew that was where I would find the missing pieces to the puzzle of my past. So far, I only knew three things for sure. Number one: I knew that Gogol was a Russian name. Number two: I had a vision not long ago, kind of like a dream, where I saw a huge primitive rocket with four Earthling letters—CCCP—on it, blasting off from a planet that looked a lot like Earth. And number three: I knew the Russians had a big space exploration program back in the 1970s. I knew that because on my very first trip to Earth, I found time to read through a bunch of books in the McClean High School library. Even though I'd forgotten a lot of what I tried to absorb that day, some bits and pieces have come back to me—including stuff about this place called Russia.

But I still didn't know how to get there. All I knew for sure was that I had to get out of this steep, narrow valley. So I started taking giant steps up the side of the hill.

"Baaa," the four-legged fur balls Xela called "sheep" jeered as I walked by.

"Baa, baa, bah humbug to you too," I said. "I've had enough rudeness from Rubi to last me all day, thank you."

"Baaa," another one teased. I started to give it a dirty look, but stopped suddenly. This one was different. Really different. All the other sheep I could see—and there were a lot of them—were white. But this one was black. I liked him instantly. He dared to be different. I wanted to communicate with him.

"Excuse me," I said, softly. "Can you show me how to get to Russia?"

The sheep nodded, let out a long "baaa," and started to run up the hill. I knew instantly that this kindred spirit wanted me to follow him. I hopped over the low stone wall that separated us, and ran after him.

The other sheep scattered in every direction as the two of us followed a zigzag path up the slope. The black sheep was a much better climber than I was. He got to the crest of the hill and waited.

Huffing and puffing, I finally caught up to him. I followed his gaze to the other side of the mountain. What I saw took what was left of my breath away. There before me were rolling green hills that stretched as far as the eye could see. They were dotted with trees, bushes, and fluffy white sheep. A free-form pattern of low rock walls crisscrossed the hills and linked them together like a crazy quilt. Small gray stone houses were set along a ribbon of dirt road that traced the hills and valleys. And as my eyes roamed closer to where I stood, I saw a scene below me that seemed magical.

A large gathering of humans was having some kind of party. Some were standing still, while others had arranged themselves in little groups, and were hopping up and down on one foot. Marvelous sounds drifted up to me on a gentle breeze. Voices, laughter, and strange, lilting music. I was so excited, I could barely speak. "Mr. Black Sheep," I said. "Are these Russians?" But the sheep didn't answer. He just yanked a tuft of grass from between two rocks and started to chew.

"I know you can understand me," I said, cupping his head in my hands and looking him straight in the eye. "Please, you can't leave me like this. You must tell me. Make it one 'baaa' for yes, two for no. Okay?"

The sheep wiggled away and bobbed his head. I wasn't sure if that meant he understood my instructions, or if he was looking for more grass, but I pressed on. "Now tell me. Are these Russians?"

The sheep raised his head and blinked his eyes.

"Come on. One 'baaa' for yes, two for no." But the sheep didn't say a thing. He jerked his head to the side and ran off down the hill.

After I knew I'd seen the last of the sheep, I flipped the collar of my jacket up, so it covered the scaly green Alzorian skin on the back of my neck, and made my way down the hill toward the gathering.

As I got close to the crowd, a giant of a man—not as tall as Rubi, but still huge—came over to me. He had long, scraggly, orange-red hair and millions of funny little pale red dots all over his skin. His eyes were blue, but not the deep, dark blue you see on the one-eyed Jinkos from Fester. These were light blue, almost green. And although his expression looked angry, his eyes seemed to smile. In some ways he reminded me of the first Goner we'd ever found on RU1:2., Noss-Mott, Thomas Jefferson, as the locals called him. I wondered if, by some miracle, I'd stumbled upon another Goner.

Until I looked down. This giant man, in fact all the men, were wearing skirts with the same colorful right-angle pattern as the boy at the lake. And any being from the Planetary Union can tell you that right angles aren't natural. Even worse, they slowly suck the energy right out of you. I could hear the Grand DOO-DUH's words of wisdom echoing in my head: "The shortest distance between two points is a curve."

53

"What's your business here, Englishman?" he asked.

"I'm not called Englishman. My name is Gogol."

"Well, I can see you're no Scottish Highlander, dressed like that," the man said. "And we Scots are none too trusting of the English. They've run roughshod over us for centuries."

"Ouch," I said, thinking this guy didn't look bad for being so old and run over.

"Ouch, indeed, laddie," the giant man laughed. "I be called Freddy McFreckle. If you're not an Englishman, then what are you?"

"I think I'm Russian," I said.

"Aye, I be rushing too, now that you mention it," the man said.

"You're Russian?" I exclaimed. I couldn't believe it! Mr. Black Sheep came through after all!

"Aye, it's time to gather at the parade ground," he said, walking away. "Come along, if you like."

"But wait, I just need to know . . ."

"Can't wait, lad," McFreckle called over his shoulder. "The Pipe and Drum Corps is about to start playing."

I hurried to catch up with the large, skirted Earthling. "I just need to know how to get to your rocket center."

"Rock center?" the man laughed. "There's no shortage of rocks in Scotland, son. You can't drop your hat without hitting one. We have no need of keeping them in a particular center, as you say. Rocks, as you can see, are everywhere."

"Not rocks. I'm talking about . . ." then I stopped. I realized this gentle giant did not have the information

I needed. Maybe only the most important Russians knew where the rocket center was. So I said, "Take me to your leader."

"Why, I was just about to do that," Freddy McFreckle said. We walked up to a small, wise-looking older man. He had silvery hair and was leaning on a carved stick. "This is our host," he said.

"Greetings, wise one," I said. "I am . . ."

"McGogol," McFreckle said. "A visitor to our clan festival."

"Welcome to my farm, sir," the silver-haired wise man said, holding his hand out. "They call me Old McDonald."

I held out my hand. He grabbed it and old or not, he squeezed it so hard, I cried out. *"Ee-iii-ee-iii-oh!"*

Old McDonald laughed. "I like the sound of that, laddie," he said. "Could you sing it once more?"

"I'd love to," I said as I shook the pain out of my hand. "But I'm in a bit of a hurry. I'm hoping you can tell me where I can find rockets."

"Rockets?" Old McDonald repeated, scrunching up his forehead. "Why sure I can, lad."

"You can?" My heart began to race. I felt light-headed.

"Aye, I've had the rare privilege of seeing them meself," he said with a far-away look. "And a grand sight it is, too. A fantastic display of power."

"I'm sure it is."

"Rockets!" he shouted, looking skyward. His arm swept through the air.

"Yes! Yes!" I said.

"Exploding in midair!"

"Yea- . . . huh?"

"Lighting the night sky with blue, white, and red fireworks," he said. "The people, cheering with delight."

"Fireworks?"

"Aye, now that was something special," Old McDonald said, bringing his eyes down to look at me. "I haven't thought about that in years. Only one place to see a sight like that. Edinburgh castle, on the queen's birthday. But alas, that's months from now."

My heart sunk. "So that's it?" I croaked. "No *big* rockets?"

McFreckle looked puzzled. "Well, we do plan to have a bonfire."

"That's nice," I muttered, kicking one of the stones that poked up everywhere from the earth around me. McFreckle had no idea what I meant. I should have known better than to think I could just walk off and find the answers I was looking for.

Just then drums started beating and the incredible sounds I'd heard before filled my ears. I looked over at the life forms making the music. Several stood with sticks in each hand beating out a gentle rhythm on drums that hung from their shoulders. Others were more original. They were making music by blowing on tubes and flapping one arm up and down, letting sound escape from their armpits.

The crowd of men and women, all dressed in their bright costumes, began to laugh and dance around Old McDonald's farm.

It was a joyous celebraton. And I didn't have anything worth celebrating. I turned my back on the little party and slowly began the long walk back over the hill to Loch Ness. Their sad, bleating music matched my mood.

It was obvious to me now that I was never going to get to Russia. Never going to get to the truth.

The late afternoon sun slowly sank behind the hills, taking with it all my hopes of ever finding out who I was. As I felt the disappointment and frustration well up inside of me. I leaned back, turned my face to the setting sun and let out my pain. *"Ee-iii-ee-iii-ohhh!"* I cried.

11

Xela Zim Bareen

Arms and I followed the golfers from flag ten to eighteen, but somehow this game didn't add up. First, they'd go to a lot of trouble to hit the little white ball into the hole. Then, they'd pull it right back out again. It's Earth logic, I guess, very primitive.

When they were done, we followed them up a narrow stone road to the place they called Inverness.

"Here we be," said Robert Campbell. We were standing in front of a large stone house with a sign in front that said CAMPBELL INN.

"Your house-ness?" Arms asked.

"I must say, you two are a delight. The wife will

love you! Come in! Come in!'' said Campbell as he held the door open for us.

The inside of the inn was warm and cluttered. It was lit by flickering flames set in clear jars attached to the walls. There were low ceilings, big overstuffed chairs, tables stacked with books, and lots of halls, stairways, and rooms you could explore, almost like the Tunnels. Guess that's why I instantly liked it.

Mr. Campbell directed us into a room with a long, heavy table. A woman ran up to greet us. "So, Robert, you've brought a couple more guests for dinner, have you?" she said.

"That I have, my Bonnie Lass," knobby Robby said with a smile.

"I'm Cornish," I said. "And this is my friend . . ."

"Kind-of-ish."

"Of course you are," Bonnie Lass said. "And just in time. We're delighted to have you for supper." Then she steered us toward a couple of large wooden chairs. Arms looked at me nervously.

"Xela," she whispered, as Bonnie Lass left the room. "When she said, 'Have you for supper,' you don't think she meant . . ."

"*Have* us for supper?" I replied. "Don't be silly."

Several other people soon came over and sat down, and Bonnie brought in a tray.

"Some nice warm vegetable soup to start with to-night," she said as she dipped scoops of the soupy stuff into shallow food holders and passed them around.

"See, Arms," I whispered. "Nothing to worry about."

"So far," she said. Then she pressed her lips against the dish and slurped in a huge mouthful. Her eyes got

59

big and a smile spread across her face. "MMmmm, MMmmm . . . good!" she proclaimed.

The man directly across from us started to chuckle. "Please don't think me rude," he said. "It's just that I've never seen a pair quite like you. You are clearly twins. You look exactly the same, except I noticed your kilts are quite odd."

"Yes," said Arms. "One polka-dot. One striped. You like them?"

His eyes twinkled. "Very much. In fact, you remind me of two characters I wrote about in a book."

"Is that so?" I said.

"Yes, Tweedle Dee and Tweedle Dum," he answered.

"Did you say Tweezles?" Arms exclaimed. "Like the Tweezles from planet Plinter?"

I gave Arms a little kick under the table. The man looked confused. "No, my Tweedles, Dee and Dum, live in a place called Wonderland."

"I'm surprised you haven't heard of it," Lister said. "This is Lewis Carroll, the author. How is the book doing, Lewis?"

"Very well, as a matter of fact. I have more *Alice in Wonderland* stories planned. But for now, I've come to relax and enjoy the Scottish Highlands."

"Alice in Wonderland?" I asked.

"It's a marvelous story," Lewis said, "if I do say so myself. All about a little girl named Alice who falls down a rabbit hole and discovers a world unlike any known before."

"Aha!" Arms said to me. "Sound familiar? An underground world? Entered through holes?"

"Arms," I whispered in her ear. "Don't be silly.

Lister told us the holes were put there for playing the game called golf.''

"A cover-up," she scoffed.

Lewis spoke again. "And how about you, Dr. Lister? How is your work at the Glasgow hospital going?"

"Very well, really," he said enthusiastically. "So well that some people find it hard to believe."

"What do you mean?" I asked.

"Well, you see, I've managed to cut the number of people dying from infections in my hospital by nearly seventy percent in the first year," Lister said proudly.

"Seventy percent!" Mr. Campbell said. "That's amazing."

"It truly is," Lister continued. "I owe much of the success to a certain scientist in Paris who . . ."

"A scientist in Paris?" I asked. "That wouldn't happen to be Louis Pasteur, would it?"

Lister stared at me for a long moment. "Yes, that's exactly who it is. How did you know? His work is only just beginning to be widely known."

"I get around," I said. "I was there when he tried out his cure for rabies."

"Rabies? There is no cure for rabies!" Lister exclaimed. *Oh-oh,* I thought, *I've blown it this time.*

"Umm, excuse me, but what year is it?" I asked weakly.

"1866, of course," Lewis said. Well, that explained it. When Rubi and I had gone on our mission to find Mission Specialist Whagg, also known as Louis Pasteur, it was the year 1888, twenty-two years in Earth's future.

"Of course there's no cure for rabies," I said, trying to cover up. "But Pasteur thinks there will be someday."

"That would be a miracle," Robert Campbell said.

"True, and if a cure is to be found, I wager Pasteur will be the one to find it," Lister said. "He has already shown that germs can travel through the air and get passed on by touch or dirty surgical instruments. That's why I insist that the hospital and everything in it be scrubbed clean every day."

"Every day? That's a bit much," said Robert.

"Not if a life can be saved. And that's not all. Doctors and nurses must wash their hands often, wear clean clothes, and all equipment must be sterilized before every use."

"Really, Joseph," said Lewis. "No wonder people are attacking you. Talk about an idea that will *never* catch on."

Lister looked hurt, but Bonnie Lass smoothed it all over. Putting a plate down in front of everyone at the table, she said, "Let's eat up now. We have lovely Cornish pasties, to start."

I could feel the blood drain from my face. I was barely breathing. Little droplets of water trickled down my forehead. *Arms may have been right after all!* I thought. Trust me, it's a bad sign on any planet when your name matches the name of the food on your plate. "Excuse me," I squeaked, "I think I have to go now."

"You can't leave now, laddie," Robert boomed out. "Mrs. Campbell has been chopping and stuffing these marvelous pasties all day long. One of my favorites. But if it's not yours, I urge you to be patient. The best is yet to come, for tonight's the night for haggis!"

Arms leaned over and whispered, "Who's Haggis?"

"I don't know who he is, but I hope they treat him better than Cornish," I said, pushing my plate away.

62

Arms and I stood up, intending to leave. But Robert blocked our way. "Never mind lads, sit back down, I'll do the honors," he said. Then he announced, "It's time to pipe in the haggis!"

Pipe the Haggis? I thought. I couldn't even begin to imagine what kind of torture that must be. "Arms," I whispered urgently. "We have to get out of here! Now!"

12

Rubidoux

As I watched Gogol disappear over the top of the hill, I swore I'd never do anything with him again. Every time we're supposed to work together, he goes off on his own and does something stupid. Then it's up to me to get him out of trouble and save the mission. *Well, no more,* I told myself.

After all, this was my last journey to Earth too. Was I getting any closer to finding Rebecca or figuring out what a call was? No. Was I in the middle of an exciting mission on a war-torn planet? No. I was stuck by the side of a peaceful lake waiting for She-Rak. Waiting for Arms. Waiting for Xela. *Not* waiting for Gogol. Yippee. Sitting around bored like that, my mind began to wander. That's when it hit me. I was sitting on top of something big. Really big!

Jackie had called the lake a "lock," as in Lock Ness. According to my pan-tawky, a lock keeps things in. So, I reasoned, maybe once you fall in this lake, you're locked in. Kind of like the gloss-bogs on my home planet of Douxwhop. They look like a puddle of clear liquid, but if you step on them . . . well, you get the idea. So, if She-Rak slipped into the lock-lake, he might be trapped down there! My antennae were swirling with excitement. Except that, as a human, I didn't have any. I reached up and touched my head. My hair was practically standing straight up. I was on to something. I was sure of it.

I ran to the water's edge and tried to look in. It was dark and murky. Slammed shut. Couldn't see a thing. I thought about jumping in for an oh-no second. But I wouldn't be much help to anyone if I got locked in the water too. So I sat back down to keep watch. Whatever was being kept down there couldn't stay trapped forever. I hoped.

But nothing unusual happened. Nothing. Not even a slight wind disturbed the water's surface. The only thing that seemed to be moving was Earth's pitiful Class 7 star. It was steadily getting lower and lower on the horizon. Things began to take on weird, shadowy shapes. The feeling in the air was . . . well, strange. Not at all like anything I'd sensed on Earth before. I felt completely alone. Isolated. Helpless.

Then I saw it. At least, I thought I saw something. It was hard to say in the deepening gloom. Just as the sun sank behind the hills, its golden rays reflected off a wet, jewel-colored trail. A slime trail! A She-Rak-type slime trail! I jumped up and ran over to it. *Splat!* Down I went. *Yeech!* I was covered in dripping slime, but *so* happy. No one but She-Rak would have left anything that gross behind! With my eyes, I followed the slime trail. . . .

I was right! She-Rak was locked in the lake! I had to help him. I had to somehow go out on the water, find him and pull him out. I ran over to Jackie's flat-bottomed wooden floater, pushed it into the water, and jumped in. *Whoa!* The thing rocked back and forth, almost tipping over. I sat down and waited for the rocking to stop. Now I was sure we had landed in a primitive time period. There were no Gravitational Balancers to keep the thing steady.

Once things settled back down, I picked up the sticks I'd seen Jackie use to move the floater. I dipped one in the water on one side, then the other on the other side. Nothing happened. So I pulled on one of the sticks. At least that got me moving. But instead of moving forward, I was going in a tight little circle. I pulled on the other one and headed in a circle in the other direction. I pulled harder and the circles got tighter. I stood up and tried pushing one stick while pulling the other. The float jiggled and bobbed around as the circles got smaller and smaller.

I was getting dizzy, spinning around while violently rocking back and forth. My head was swirling. My stomach was speaking a whole other language. *That's it!* I thought. *I'm not going anywhere.* I stopped and sat down. That's when I noticed that I'd somehow managed to move to the middle of the lake. I could barely even see the shore. To make things worse, it was dark already. It made me mad at Gogol all over again. If he had been with me, as he should have been, there wouldn't be a problem. I would have just thrown him overboard and made him push me to shore. But no, he just had to leave me alone. In the dark. In the cold. In the middle of . . . "AAAAHHH!" I screamed.

Something was moving. Right below me. Making huge swells in the water. One moment everything had been calm. Now the water was bucking and rocking like there was some huge monster struggling to get free. Could it be . . . could it be . . .

"She-Rak?" I stood up and started screaming over and over. "She-Rak! Over here, buddy. Come on, old boy." I stabbed one of the sticks into the water and wiggled it around. "Grab hold, She-Rak. I'll pull you out!" But there was nothing. Everything was quiet again. Except for me. I was loud. Until I got tired of yelling at the nothingness around me.

Maybe I imagined the whole thing, I thought. I sat back down, feeling discouraged. I could no longer see the shore of the lake. It was totally dark. I was cold. Fog was closing in around me. The push-pull sticks made a splash as I plopped them into the water, gave one a yank and started moving in a circle—again. *Well, at least I'm not bored any more,* I thought. *Now I'm terrified.* Be careful what you wish for.

13

Arms Akimbo

Light and heat from the next room poured in as a door swung open. There stood Robert, and strapped to him was a soft bag with wooden tubes jutting out of it. He drew a deep breath and slowly blew into one of the tubes. As he did, the bag-thing puffed up and seemed to come to life. It made a sound somewhere between a low moan and a squeal. Then, he squeezed it under his arm! The bag began to scream!

"You're hurting it!" I yelled, putting my hands over my ears. But no one seemed to care. Everyone else had huge smiles on their faces.

"Ah! Nothing like piping in the haggis, is there?" Lister said as we watched Knobby-Kneed Robby run his fingers over the pipes and make sad, whining sounds.

"Aye. Nothing like it," Xela agreed.

"That poor screaming bag-thing is Mr. Haggis?" I asked. No one answered me. But Xela leaned over and whispered in my ear.

"Arms, you're making a little bit of a scene. Mission specialists are supposed to blend in. Pretend you like the noise." She was right, of course. I took my hands off my ears, put a toothy smile on my face, and showed it to everyone at the table. "That's much better," Xela said with a smile.

All of a sudden, Bonnie Lass Campbell came through the door, holding a steaming something high on a silver dish. Everyone "oohhed" and "ahhhed" as she set it in the center of the table. It was a large, roundish, pale, moist blob of . . .

"Haggis!" Robert cheered.

"So this is haggis?" I said. "Looks like a basketball that's been bleached, boiled, and run over." Then, remembering I was supposed to blend in, I added, "Yum."

"Dr. Lister." Bonnie smiled. "You're a surgeon. You carve." Everyone laughed.

"Don't think me rude," Arms said. "But what's in it?"

"Are you sure you're a Scot?" Lewis asked. "It's the national dish!"

"It's haggis, lads," Bonnie said patiently. "The finest sheep innards, all chopped up and mixed with onion and oatmeal . . ."

"Steam-cooked inside a sheep's stomach. Give me a thick slice, Joseph," Lewis said.

I suddenly felt woozy. My head was spinning, and I couldn't catch my breath. I pushed my chair away from the table. "Sorry, I just remembered. I already ate. Back at the dump."

"Me too," Xela said. "Maybe I'll just have a taste of the white stuff in the bowl."

"Aye," said Bonnie. "Bashed neeps and tatties coming up." She splatted a huge spoonful on Xela's plate. I gave Lister a worried look.

"Mashed turnips and potatoes," he whispered.

They didn't look so bad. "I'll have that too," I said, pulling myself together. I decided it was time to get to the point. "Mr. Campbell, you said you knew all about clans, right?"

"Yes, indeed. What do you want to know?"

"We're looking for someone who may have gone off to find the Rak clan," Xela said. "Ever heard of it?"

"Rak?" repeated Campbell. "I'm afraid not." No one at the table had heard of a clan called Rak, but they all joined in trying to name every clan name that started with an "r" to see if one sounded close. There was Robertson and Ross. Rose and Rollo. Ramsay, Ranald, Ruthven, and Rattray.

"Rat-ray?" Xela said. "That's sort of close."

"Rattray and Rak are not the same thing, Cornish," I said. "Face it, we struck out. No luck. We should be going."

"And just where are you headed this time of night?" Bonnie asked. "It's pitch dark outside."

"We're staying down by the lake," Xela said.

"I wouldn't get too close to the lake at night if I were you," Robert said mysteriously. "Could be dangerous."

70

"What do you mean?" I asked, sliding a mouthful of starchy soft stuff down my throat.

"Robert is referring to the so-called monster of Loch Ness, of course," Lewis said.

Lister looked uncomfortable. "Must we go on about that topic again tonight?" he said to no one in particular.

"If they're going down to the lake, they should know the risks," Robert said firmly. Then he looked at us and went on. "The Loch Ness Monster is a huge creature that rules the lake. It's very powerful, but also sly. It has only been seen by a few people."

"At least, they claim to have seen it," Lewis Carroll said sarcastically. "The existence of this terrible monster, as you call it, has never been proven."

"Then how do you explain all the sightings, Lewis?" Bonnie asked. "The stories go back for centuries."

"My feeling is most of these reports are honest mistakes," said Lewis. He took a huge bite of haggis and kept talking. Gross. "Someone sees a log floating in the lake, they say it's the monster. A school of fish disturbs the calm waters, they say it's the monster. Others are either daft or liars. Or maybe cleverly trying to create a legend so tourists will come stay at their inns."

Robert looked at his wife, who quickly looked away. Something was going on between them. Maybe he was one of those innkeepers. Finally, he spoke. "I have seen the monster with my own eyes, Lewis," he said haltingly. "And it is real."

"Is that so?"

"Aye, it's true. I don't admit it often though. It can be an embarrassment."

"Tell us what you saw," Xela said.

"It was a clear day, the water was calm. I was in

71

my boat, fishing near the ruins of Urquart Castle. There the lake is especially deep. Suddenly, for no apparent reason, the monster rose out of the water and charged toward me. I grabbed the oars and managed to get out of the way, just a moment before it would have crashed into me.''

"And why do you think it did that?'' I asked.

"I suspect it was hungry,'' Robert answered. "I have no doubt that if I'd fallen in the water, she'd eaten me.''

"Whoa, what did it look like?'' Xela asked.

"It was a fearsome beastie, I'm afraid. A huge body with a long neck. Dark leathery skin. And a small head fitted with enormous jaws and two stubby horns.''

Lewis gently shook his head and smiled. "You've been awfully quiet, Dr. Lister. What do you think about all this?''

Lister answered slowly. "I think all this talk of a monster is dangerous.''

"Dangerous?'' I asked.

"Dangerous for the creature, of course,'' Lister said. "If there is one, that is. If we keep talking about it, more and more people will come to try and capture or even kill her. And that would be a tragedy.''

"Better it than us,'' Bonnie hissed. "You can't even sit by the side of the lake at night without taking your life in your hands.''

"What do you mean?'' Arms asked.

"My friend Catherine says the monster rises out of the lake and eats creatures that venture too close to the shore at night.''

"That is ridiculous!'' Lister protested.

"Tell that to Mrs. Robertson,'' Bonnie cried. "The poor dear lost a calf to the monster.''

"It eats at the caf?" I asked, remembering the strange dining ritual Rubi had told us about at an Earth place called "high school."

"It eats what it wants," Bonnie said in a low voice. "Any living thing that's unlucky enough to fall in the water or stand too close to the shore will likely be the monster's next meal."

My head jerked over to face Xela. "She-Rak!" I shouted.

"Gogol!" she said.

"Rubi!" we both screamed, jumping up from the table.

"Stop!" Bonnie said. "You can't leave now! You haven't had your dessert. Sponge pudding."

"Sheesh! Is there an animal on this planet they *don't* eat?" I mumbled to Xela.

"Sorry, but our friends may be in trouble," Xela said as we stood up.

"But I will take some haggis to go, please," I said, wrapping a piece in a napkin.

"Arms, what are you doing?" Xela whispered.

"Shh . . . Bottom Feeder bait," I muttered. Then to the table, I said, "Thanks so much for the lovely stories."

"And the mushed up beepers and natters," Xela added.

"Yeah, the food was, uh, interesting," I said to Bonnie. "But, let me give you a word of advice, Mrs. Campbell."

"Yes?"

"Stick to soup."

14

Rubidoux

I spun around in a fog for what seemed an eternity. First turning this way, then the other. I was tired. Weak from hunger. Cold. Wet. Lost. *Thud!* I hit something. Hard. It was the shore! What luck! I somehow ended up back where I started. I jumped out of the floater and pulled it up onto the land. *As if Gogol wasn't enough trouble,* I thought. *Now She-Rak has to make my life miserable. I can't wait until I get my hands on . . .*

"Who?" a voice called out.

"She-Rak, that's who," I answered before I realized that whoever was talking to me would have had to read my thoughts to ask that question.

"Who's there?" I cried.

"Who?" the ghostlike voice cried again.

"I asked you first, mind-reader!" I said. "Answer me!"

"Who?"

"Rubidoux, that's who," I spat out, turning to face the direction I thought the voice was coming from. Whatever it was had a funny voice, as if most of its body was nose and the sound just rippled up through it. The thought of facing a mind-reading, who-calling, walking nose-creature face to face on a dark, foggy night, after all I'd been through already, made me just the smallest bit nervous. Then I had a thought.

"Arms," I sighed. "Is that you?"

"Who?" came the cry.

"Stop it," I shrieked. I was hoping it was Arms pulling one of her ridiculous practical jokes. But no matter what, I had to keep calm. So I swallowed hard and decided to ignore the Who Nose for now. "Go ahead and who-who all you want," I called. "I'm not playing anymore!"

"Who?"

"Very funny," I muttered. Then I sat down to figure out my next move. The first thing I had to take care of was my Earthling body. It was freezing! Being stuck on "cold" was a whole new sensation. In my Douxwhopian body, my blood just warmed or cooled to match the outside temperature. I'd never stayed cold this long before. I never realized before how bad Earthlings had it! I needed a heat source and fast. My body was already covered with tiny little bumps and I was shaking so badly I thought I might fly apart. *Fire!* I thought. *But how?*

I gathered some flammable dry sticks of wood and

piled them up in front of me. But no matter how hard I concentrated, I couldn't make them burst into flames. If I'd had my tentacles, I could have focused enough energy on them, no problem. But here on Earth, in a Scottish body, I had to find another way.

Friction! I thought, remembering my Crude Molecular Interactions class. I had never tried it before, but now was a pretty good time to start. I picked up two sticks and started rubbing them together as fast as I could. Nothing. I worked harder. Rubbing. Rubbing. Rubbing. Finally, I could feel them getting warm. I thought I saw a tiny wisp of smoke! And where there's smoke, there's . . . nothing. No flame. No spark. No nothing. I threw the sticks down, mad. This was not my day. But I did feel warmer. I calculated that I must have worked the sticks hard enough to transfer their stored energy to me. Amazing! What a planet!

Even more amazing, the who-ing had stopped. I didn't know whether to be happy or sad. If it was a hostile creature, I was glad it was gone. But I was still hoping it was really Arms and Xela.

"Who!" I called. Silence. I tried again. A great, huge bird flew out of the trees near me and swooped just a bit too close for comfort. I would have complained, but I was distracted by the sound of bushes rustling up on the hill.

Two can play this game. I decided to sneak up on the Who Nose, or whatever it was, and scare it away. Crouched down low, I began to make my way up the hill, being sure not to make a sound. I got closer. Closer. Nearly on top of it. Then, at just the right moment, I jumped up and threw myself at it!

"Uuumph," it cried as we both fell to the ground.

"Don't you mean 'who?' " I sneered.

"You know who!" it shouted.

"Gogol?"

"You were expecting someone else?"

"No, but . . . I thought you'd be in Russia."

"So did I." Gogol sighed as we helped each other up. "But here I am. No Russia. No rockets. No reasons."

"I'm sorry to hear that," I said.

"Forget it," Gogol said sadly. "Let's just get out of here. Where's She-Rak? Did he come back?"

"Not exactly," I said. "But I think I know where he is."

"So what are we waiting for? Let's go get him."

"One little problem," I admitted. "Someone locked him in the lake and threw away the key."

15

Arms Akimbo

It was dark. Really dark. Like the darkest part of the deepest Tunnel back on Roma. Even the night-light from Earth's one moon was hidden by large dark clouds. Xela and I were carefully and slowly making our way down a majorly bumpy dirt road. Below, the lake was covered with fog.

"We're lucky the Campbells let us borrow this fire-in-a-bowl thing Bonnie Lass called a 'lantern,'" Xela said, holding the flame holder up high. "Otherwise, we wouldn't be able to see a thing."

"No kidding," I said. "Dark. Foggy. Cold. Scary."

"Feels just like our favorite place back home," Xela joked.

"Xela," I said as the road started to level out. "Do you think there really is a monster in the lake?"

"I don't know, Arms. There may be a creature, but it's probably harmless. Then again . . ."

"Right. We can't be too sure. I mean, this is Earth, one of the more violent of the lesser-known planets."

"Don't remind me," said Xela. We walked without talking for a while. That's when I thought I heard something. I moved closer to Xela.

"What was that?" she whispered.

"I don't know. What did it sound like to you?"

"Sounded like someone on the road behind us." We stopped and turned around. Xela held the lantern up high. "She-Rak? Is that you?" But there was no answer.

"Gogol? Rubi?" I said. Nothing. "Robert? Joseph? Bonnie? Lewis?"

"It's probably no one, Arms. I bet we're just a little jumpy after all that monster talk."

"Sure. That's it," I said, as we started walking again. "But we don't need to worry. If there is a monster, the haggis in my pocket will scare him off."

"Why do you think I keep walking ahead?" Xela smiled. We hadn't gotten much farther when I heard the sound again. A kind of shuffling noise. Xela shot me another worried look. "Arms, tell me you're the one doing that."

"Xela, I swear by the six stars of Erin, it wasn't me."

"So what do we do?"

"Keep walking, like nothing's wrong. I'll start to count, and when I get to three, we stop and listen. Ready? One thousand, thirty-two point six, *three*!" We both came to a halt. There it was! The unmistakable sound of another set of feet stopping just after we did.

"Could it be an echo?" Xela asked.

"No way," I breathed. "Xela, I don't know who's sneaking up behind us or why, but we have to lose them. Agreed?"

"Agreed."

"So get ready, we're about to make a run for it."

"Run?" Xela said, sounding worried. "Run where? How do we . . . what do we . . ."

"Shhh! Hand me the lantern. Ready? Tense . . . release!" We took off running down the road in the dark. Fast—as fast as we could. I turned the flame in the lantern down, covered the rest of its light with one arm, and grabbed Xela with the other. Two more arms would have made this a lot easier, but I did the best I could. "Hurry, Xela. Stay with me."

"I can't see!"

"Here we go!" I yelled, as I led her off the road, through some bushes, and up a steep hill.

"We can hide here," I panted, pulling Xela behind a huge boulder.

"Whew!" Xela said as we tumbled to the ground. "Did we lose them?"

"Only one way to find out," I said through gasps. I stood up and looked down at the road through trees and bushes. Moonlight, finally breaking through the clouds, gave me a pretty good view. Nothing. "I think they're gone, whoever or whatever they were."

"Good," Xela said, relieved. "Now we can relax. AAARGH!"

I turned back to where Xela was sitting. Actually, where she had been sitting. She was gone! "This is no time to play sneak-and-peek, Xela," I said. "Come out, come out, wherever you . . . uh-oh." I felt the ground beneath my feet shift. Sink. Crumble. Collapse!

"Xela?" I yelled as I fell into a hole. "Wait for me, Xela. Here I come! Wheeeeee!"

16

Arms Akimbo

I was barreling straight down through the dark at what felt
to me like close to P-force speed. "Yippee!" I squealed.

"Oooff!" Xela replied as I landed right on top of
her. "Arms, is that you?"

"No. It's the Loch Ness Monster."

"It's so dark in here, it just could be. I can't see a thing."

"If you were your natural shape, Xela, you could
turn on the light in your third eye," I said fiddling with
the lantern. "Instead you're just going to have to wait
till I get this lantern thing lit again."

"Where do you think we are?" whispered Xela.

"I think we fell down a rabbit hole, like in that Lewis
guy's story about Alice."

"That would have to be one big rabbit."

I gently stood the lantern up on a part of ground that felt level and reached in my pocket for a stick of fire. "Xela, do you remember what Mr. Campbell did to make this catch-on-fire stick thing work?"

"I think so," she said. "You strike it."

"Figures."

"No, I mean scrape it across something rough."

"Here goes." I scraped the stick across the rock, and to my amazement, it lit! "I did it! Score one for primitive technology."

"Be careful, Arms," said Xela as she lifted up the glass jar part of the lantern. "Let me help." Then she pulled up a piece of rope that was coated with some goop. As soon as I touched the match to it, the rope stuff caught fire and glowed brightly.

"Success!" I hooted. "Are we good or what?"

"Yeah, we're great," Xela said. "Now let's use all this greatness to find a way out of here." By the soft light of the lantern, we could see that we were in an underground tunnel of some kind. It was craggy and narrow. Water dripped down the walls. Parts of plants dangled from the ceiling.

"Why don't we just go back up the rabbit hole?" I asked.

Xela held the light up. The hole we fell through had dropped us into a cave. "Looks like the hole is too far away for us to reach, even standing on each other's shoulders. I say we follow this path. It's bound to come out somewhere."

"Path" was putting it kindly. It was really just a sort of incredibly skinny ledge that only went off in one direction. "After you, Alice," I snorted.

Even though it was dark and we were basically completely lost, I wasn't scared because it was so much like the Tunnels back home. "Xela, what do you think the chances are that we'll run into maintenance breffels or Scrapebotz?"

"Pretty unlikely, but I did just have a thought. If there is a monster in the lake, this would be a great place for it to hide."

"Gee, just when I was starting to have fun."

"Shhh!" Xela said. "What was that?" We both crouched down. I couldn't hear anything above the pounding of my heart and the drip, drip, splat sounds coming off the walls. So I stood back up. That's when I heard it. A hopelessly sad wailing.

"Sounds like the whining of a huge creature," Xela whispered.

"With a really bad case of indigestion," I added. "Must have eaten the haggis."

"Let's see if we can get a look at it."

"I have a better idea. Let's not." But it was too late. Xela was already hurrying down the passageway toward the sound. And she had the light. So I followed. "Okay, Xela, but don't let whatever it is see you."

As we got closer, the beast-with-a-bellyache idea just didn't seem to fit. "Now it sounds more like wind whistling through the rocks," I said.

"But it's playing a tune," Xela pointed out. She was right.

"What a country!" I exclaimed. "Even the wind knows how to play 'Old Lang Swine'!"

"That's not the wind, Arms. It's bag-o-pipes."

"Pipes-a-rama! We must be close to getting out of

here." Then I grabbed the lantern out of Xela's hand and ran down the trail.

"Arms, slow down!" I heard Xela call. But I didn't want to. I didn't want to admit it, but I was getting just the teeniest bit uncomfortable trapped in that underground maze. All I wanted to do was get out.

Just one more ridiculously narrow passageway and I'll be seeing moonlight, I told myself as I headed toward a blast of cold air. I was so excited to be coming out of this place into . . . into . . . what?

"Arms!" Xela called as she ran up beside me. "Why were you . . . whoa! Where are we? Outside?"

"I don't think so," I said. "I think we're in a huge, gigunda, mega-size cavelike thing." I could feel the tiny muscles in my human eyes cranking my irises open wider. As my eyes adjusted I could just barely make out the wall on the opposite side of the cave. Then I heard the bag-o-pipes again. Very close.

"Cover the lantern, Arms. Get down!" Xela urged.

I shoved the lantern behind me and leaned against the cold stone wall. "Xela, *look!*" I gasped. A light was moving toward us! It was just on the other side of the huge rock we were crouching behind. On the far wall, I could make out a gigantic silhouette. "What is it?" I asked.

"I'm not sure," Xela muttered. "Based on its shadow, I'd say it's a big two-legged creature with either monster-sized bagpipes or a row of spiny-things running down its back."

"It's a giant, all right," I said. "And, I don't know how to tell you this, but it's about to find us."

It was true. There was nowhere to run. Nowhere to hide. We were about to be discovered and probably eaten. *What's with Scotland, anyway?* I wondered. Monsters in the lake. Tiny creatures in underground cities. Colossal rabbit holes that lead to mysterious worlds. Man-eating musical giants.

"Hey, Xela!" I whispered. "I'm really starting to like this place!"

17

Gogol

"What do you mean someone locked him in the lake?" I asked Rubi. "What are you talking about?"

"Our Earthling sample, Jackie, called this lake *Lock Ness* for one very good reason," Rubi explained as we headed down the hill to the shore. "Anything that falls in, stays in. Permanently."

"You think She-Rak fell in?"

"Slimed in, really," Rubi pointed out. "I found his slime trail and it ran straight into the lock-lake."

That worried me. "Can he breathe under water?" I asked.

"Hey, he's a Bottom Feeder. They can adapt to anything."

Rubi's logic seemed a little twisted to me, but one thing was for sure. She-Rak was in the lock-lake, and it was up to us to save him. "So Rubi," I said. "How do you suggest we get She-Rak out?"

"I don't know," he said. "I already tried going out onto the lake and calling for him. No luck."

"What do you think about fishing?" I suggested.

"Gogol, I know She-Rak may not be our favorite life form on Roma, but after we came all this way for him . . ."

"Hey, Rubi, She-Rak helped to save my life. There's no way I'd abandon him. Not now. Not ever."

"So what are you talking about?"

"Fishing for She-Rak. Xela told me all about the way the crew did it on Columbus's ship, the *Santa Maria.* The technology is primitive, but she claimed it worked. You start by tying a rope to a pole."

"But we don't . . ."

"Then we attach some kind of bait . . ." I continued.

"We don't . . ."

"And when She-Rak sees it, he'll come to the surface and we'll all go home."

Rubi laughed. "That is a very nice plan, Gogol, but I'm afraid you've forgotten one thing."

"What?"

"WE DON'T HAVE ANY OF THAT STUFF!"

"Sure we do," I said as I calmly reached into my pockets. "Let's see, here's the WAT-Man, of course. Then there's rope, some emergency food pellets, mini-light sticks, my diary . . ."

"I had no idea you had all that stuff with you!" Rubi exclaimed.

"Sure. Be prepared, that's my motto." I laughed as

I kept unloading my pockets. "Here's a reflective surface, a laser cutter, some HEET . . ."

"You brought Heat Energy Emission Tablets?"

"Sure, want some?"

"Are you kidding?" Rubi said. "I tried to start a fire before. I'm freezing. My legs especially."

"Rubi, you *are* wearing a skirt. But here, you want heat, you have HEET." I set the stored energy pill on the ground, and it instantly transformed into a glowing ball of radiant heat.

"Ahhh!" Rubi said, standing close to the source. "Much better."

While Rubi warmed himself, I got busy tying my entire collection of odds and ends to the rope, so they would hang one after the other. Our line had to look packed with edible junk if we wanted to attract a Bottom Feeder.

"As soon as these food pellets hit the water, they'll puff up and start to melt," I explained, holding the string up high and admiring my work. "I also attached my mini-light stick to the end of the rope to try to grab his attention."

"It looks so disgusting, it's guaranteed to draw a Bottom Feeder," Rubi agreed.

"Yeah? Well, a lot of this is good junk," I said. "And I want it back. Especially my alien decoder ring and the see-around-corners light tube."

"No problem, let's go," Rubi said as we got into Jackie's little float. "You drive."

"Okay," I agreed, dipping the two sticks into the water.

Rubi laughed. "Gogol, I can already see you're not

going to be very good at this. You've got both the sticks in the up position.''

"So?''

"So, they're push-pull sticks. You have to push on one and pull on the other. Then you can zig and zag your way along.''

Ignoring Rubi, I pulled on both sticks at once with a powerful stroke. The boat jumped forward. Then, I lifted the ends out, rotated the sticks back to the starting position, dipped them in the water and pulled a second time. Again we shot forward. Perfectly straight.

Rubi glared at me. "Show-off," he said.

"Just observant. I watched Jackie do it," I said, moving the boat steadily away from the shore with long, even strokes. "Throw the bait rope in, Rubi. We might as well be trailing it along with us.'' Rubi switched on the mini-light stick at the bottom of the rope and dropped the line into the water. I watched as it all but disappeared in the murky blackness.

"Even light gets locked up down there," Rubi observed as he tied the line to the side of the floater. "This is one strange place.''

"Quiet!'' I rasped.

Rubi looked surprised. "Don't tell me you're going to start bossing me around again.''

"Shhh! Listen," I urged, straining my ears.

Rubi was quiet for a moment, then turned to me. "What is it?'' I hesitated, then heard the sound again. Moving closer to Rubi, I whispered, "I think we're being followed.''

18

Rubidoux

Gogol stood up and leaned in the direction of the sound.
Guess he figured it would help his hearing. From the
look on his face, I could see it was definitely helping
his concentration. He was standing there. Frozen. Every
one of his Earthling-type muscles tight and ready to
spring.

"Arms?" he called out in a harsh whisper. "Is that
you?"

"She-Rak!" I yelled, hoping our missing friend
would finally show his face. We were met with dead
calm. Nothing answered. Or moved.

"What now?" I asked softly.

"I'm not sure," said Gogol. That one sentence let

me know he was pretty scared. Gogol hates to admit it when he doesn't know what to do. This place was getting to him too.

"Might as well keep moving then," I said. I dipped the pull-sticks in the water. One stroke. Two. Then I stopped and listened.

"There it is again," said Gogol. "There's definitely something or someone out there."

"A genius," I said. "Your powers of Earthly deduction have me in awe."

"Rubi, picking on me is not going to make this situation any better."

"But it might help pass the time," I joked.

"Two can play at that game," said Gogol. "Let's start with you explaining why you're always sure you know the answer, even when you're wrong!"

"I believe you're talking about you."

"You who?"

"Don't you-who me," I sneered. "I'm not putting up with any more Who Nose nonsense tonight."

"Who knows?" Gogol said.

"You know, Who Nose. Now cut it out," I said. "You're rocking the boat."

"If you're suggesting I'm upsetting the mission, I beg to differ."

"No, I mean it," I said. "Sit down; you're rocking the boat."

"Rubi," said Gogol, his voice suddenly dropping low. "I don't know how to tell you this, but it's not me."

He was right. For once. Something had hold of our bait rope and was pulling on it, making us rock back and forth. "She-Rak!" I cried. "It *must* be him!" The water all around us was moving. Bubbling. Rising. Falling.

"Come on up, She-Raa—WHOA!" yelled Gogol as he fell backward onto the bench. "Say, Rubi, did I ever mention to you that I can't swim?"

"No, but this is one heck of a time to bring it up!"

"Sorry, guess I'm a little sensitive about it. Life forms from Alzor are excellent swimmers. It's a talent you're born with when you're reptilian. But not me, of course. I got stuck with this human nose. No nose lids, just open nostrils."

"Gogol, as fascinating as it is talking about your nostrils, it's not really the time to . . . AAAAHHHHH!" I screamed as our transport nearly tipped over. The waves were powerful now. Sloshing over the sides. We were bucking up and down. Being tossed all over the place. I struggled to untie the bait line.

"Hurry Rubi! Untie that thing before he pulls us under!" Gogol screamed.

"Got it!" I said, tossing the rope into the lake. Everything suddenly went very still. "Looks like the crisis is over, Gogol. You can relax."

Suddenly a huge, dark monster with a long, snakelike neck came roaring out of the water right in front of us!

"AAAAHHHHH!" Gogol shrieked.

"Okay, that is definitely *not* She-Rak," I noted as calmly as I could. Our line of Bottom Feeder bait hung from the thing's mouth as it jerked its massive head back and forth. Then it let go of the line and sent it sailing end over end through the air.

"My alien decoder ring!" Gogol said as it flew past us.

"Never mind that stuff!" I shouted. "GET US OUT

93

OF HERE!'' Gogol grabbed the sticks and churned the water furiously. The beast arched over and plunged back into the lake, nearly crushing us as it went. I was already thanking the six stars of Erin for our escape when the waves created by its dive tossed us into the air. I held on for dear life and closed my eyes tight.

When I opened them again, I was still on board the rocking vessel, the waves were settling down and the monster was gone. So was Gogol.

19

Xela Zim Bareen

"AAARRRGGHHHH!" Arms screamed as a huge light zapped us. I closed two measly eyes and hoped the approaching giant would leave us alone. The haunting music stopped. In fact, it grew deadly quiet.

I heard footsteps coming slowly toward us. "Oh, it's you!" squealed Arms. My eyes flew open.

"Jackie?" I asked. "But you're not a giant!"

Jackie laughed. "That's just a trick of the light. The wall is so far back, my shadow makes me *look* like a giant."

"That's what I thought," I said. "But Arms, I mean Kind-of-ish, thought you were a giant, so I played along."

Jackie smiled. "Certainly, Cornish. So what are you doing in my tunnels? How did you get in?"

"Fell straight down a rabbit hole," Arms said.

"Rabbit hole?"

"We've been trying to find our way out of here and back to the lake," I added. "Can you show us the way?"

"Well, yes, I could do that. But I just got here. I won't be leaving until I visit my friend."

"You're here to visit a friend?" Arms asked.

"Underground?" I added. "In the middle of the night?"

"I know it seems odd. But . . ." said Jackie as he glanced around. "Tell you what, wait right here, and I'll come back after a couple hours and lead you out."

We were both silent. Arms looked at me. I looked at her. I knew what she was thinking, and I couldn't have agreed more. There was no way we were going to sit around waiting for hours. "Look, Jackie," Arms said. "It's none of our business why you're here, but we can't just sit doing nothing. So you go visit with whomever . . ."

"And we'll just keep looking for the exit," I finished.

"Forget you ever saw us," said Arms as she picked up the lantern and prepared to leave.

"But it's dangerous," said Jackie. "The tunnels go on forever, turning every which way. There are bottomless pits, hidden cliffs, moss-covered slippery slopes that will dump you into rushing rapids . . ."

"Sounds like home!" Arms shouted. "What are we waiting for!"

"One moment." Jackie sighed. I could see him turning something over in his mind, debating with himself.

He looked away, then looked back at us and shrugged. "If you got lost, and no one ever found you, it would be all my fault. Come on. Follow me." Then he turned and headed back toward the passageway we'd just come through.

"But that's the way back in," Arms said.

"That's because we're going to go visit my friend first, before I lead you out." Then Jackie turned to the two of us and held the lantern up high, where he could see our faces. "But first you have to promise that you will never ever tell anyone about my friend."

"I can keep a secret," I said.

"And you, Cavendish?" Jackie asked.

"Hey, any friend of yours is a friend of mine, Jack-o," Arms smiled. "Your secret will be safe with me."

Jackie smiled. "Very well then, let's get moving. I'm already late." Jackie turned and started back through the narrow passageway. Arms and I walked behind him.

"So, Jackie," Arms called. "Just who is this mysterious friend of yours?"

"I thought you would have guessed by now," he called over his shoulder as the bag-o-pipes started to softly moan.

"I have no idea," I said.

"Me either," Arms admitted.

Jackie stopped suddenly and turned to face us. "Well then," he said, "prepare yourselves. You're about to come face to face with the dreaded Loch Ness Monster."

20

Rubidoux

"Gogol!" I screamed. "Where are you?" Silence. *Oh no!* I thought. *He's trapped in the lock-lake.* I tried to remember if he could breathe liquid air, but I couldn't recall. It was terrible. All my fault. If I'd known he couldn't swim, I never would have let him come. In the dark. The fog. I would have made him wait on shore. I would have come alone.

"Uuhhhh." The sound of a faint moan reached my ears!

"Where are you?"

"Uuhhhhh." It took me a moment to figure out the moan was coming from behind the floating transport. I picked up one of the pull sticks and jammed it into the water so Gogol could grab on.

"Ooowww!"

"Oh, no!" I screamed. "Sorry, Gogol! Are you okay?" No answer! "Gogol?"

"Blub, blub, glub . . ." I figured I must have clobbered him on the head or something. I was terrified. My single heart felt like it was pounding seven hundred and twenty beats a minute. I threw down the stick and leaned over the side as far as I could. I stretched my arms out and felt Gogol floating just past my fingertips.

"Hold on, buddy!" I cried. "I'll save you." With a burst of energy, I extended my body farther out over the water. For a split moment, I felt oddly weightless. That was just before I fell face first into the freezing water and brought the boat over on top of me.

It felt as if some incredible force were holding me under the dark water. I kicked. I pulled. I thrashed around, trying to break through to the surface. *Jackie was right,* I thought. *It is a lock.* Finally, I stopped struggling so much and was relieved to find my body floating toward the surface. I came up sputtering and gasping, pulling in mountains of air in great, huge gulps. I tried to get my bearings. Where was Gogol? The transport? How far had I moved away from them? I heard a small splash and whipped my head around.

Something sitting high in the water was coming right for me. Moving silently and quickly. I didn't know what to do. Where to go. Drawing on every lesson I'd ever learned at DUH, I did the only thing that made sense in these circumstances. I panicked! Completely and utterly. I clawed at the water and screamed, "Autonomou! Bring us home! Help!" at the top of my lungs. But I knew it was hopeless. She couldn't hear me. No one could. Gogol and I were doomed.

21

Arms Akimbo

"We're going to meet the Loch Ness Monster?" I repeated.

"Jackie, you're just being funny, right?" said Xela.

Jackie smiled. "No, Nessie and I have been friends for quite some time. Ever since I stumbled onto her underground cave."

"But she's a man-eating monster!" I said.

"Arms!" said Xela.

"Oops." I shrugged. "I mean the people we met in town said that."

"All lies." Jackie sighed. "People are just afraid of what they don't understand." A little farther along, Jackie led us through a small opening in a rock wall. It was a tight squeeze, but when we wiggled through, we came out into another cave of a room. Jackie lit the end of a stick and touched the flame to lanterns that hung along the walls. When he was done, yellow light filled the cave. It was perfectly round with a dome-shaped ceiling.

"No right angles here," I said.

"What a relief," Xela agreed.

"Careful where you step," Jackie said. "I wouldn't want you to fall in!" He was standing next to a big pool of dark water that took up more than half of the room.

"Jackie," Xela said, as she looked around. "What is all this?" It was pretty amazing. Little bits and pieces of all kinds of things—sort of like what you'd expect to find on Autonomou's shelves—were lying everywhere.

"Oh, just presents I've brought for Nessie," said Jackie as he put on a paper hat. "Rings and sealing wax and other fancy stuff."

"That's so sweet," Xela cooed.

"So when do we get to see this monster?" I wanted to know.

"She'll be here soon enough," Jackie answered. "But please don't call her a monster. She's a little sensitive."

"Of course." I blushed.

"There is one more thing," he said. "There's a baby."

"A baby monster?" I blurted out.

"Kind-of-ish!" Xela said. "Sorry, sorry!"

Jackie shook his head and went on. "Yes, the Loch Ness monster has had a baby. She's quite fond of it. But . . ."

"But?" Xela asked.

"But the baby looks a little odd. I don't know why. Just try not to stare, and whatever you do, don't ask her about it."

"Of course," Xela agreed.

"Okay," I said, "but what . . ."

Suddenly the pool of water we were standing next to rose up and fell back down. Then it started churning. Thrashing. Splashing. But no monster, I mean Nessie, popped out.

Jackie smiled and shouted, "It's okay, Nessie. These are my friends!" Then he turned to us. "She's a little shy. Come on out, Nessie!"

But she didn't come out. Instead the surface of the water got totally calm. "I guess we scared her off," Xela said. "Sorry."

Just then a *huge* creature shot straight up out of the water and nearly hit the ceiling. It had a smallish oval head with two small horns and a huge blubbery body connected together by an amazingly long neck. The beast snaked its face around so it was just inches from mine. Haggis breath! *Yeech!*

"Hi," I said. "You must be Nessie. Pleased to meet you. That was some show you put on."

Nessie paddled over to Jackie. He reached up and patted her on the nose. "Hello, Nessie, sorry I'm late. I . . ."

"Jackie, look!" Xela shouted. The water right in front of her was sloshing around.

"Must be the baby!" I squealed. "Let me see!" I ran next to Xela and we both leaned over to try and get a look.

"I guess it's too shy," Xela said.

"Not really shy," Jackie said. "More like . . ." Suddenly, the baby's stubby gray tail popped up and splashed us. "Playful!" Jackie laughed. "Come on out, baby," he called. "You've had your fun."

Xela and I watched as the baby swam just under the surface to where Jackie stood, jumped out of the water and stood next to Jackie. "Baby!" Jackie cheered. "Here you are! Meet my friends."

Xela and I just stared at Baby Nessie, in total shock.

22

Rubidoux

Terrified and cold from the freezing water, I lost all sense of time. Of place. I just stopped, exhausted, and started to sink like a rock. That's when I heard a voice calling out to me from the fog. "Hello, there. Where are you?" The voice seemed very close. I started to paddle away again. Whoever had been chasing me across the water could only wish me harm.

"Where are you, boy?" It took all of my courage not to answer. I knew I had to get out of the water before I was locked up tight. Still, I didn't know if I could trust this person. What did he want from me? And what had he done with Gogol?

"Uuuuhhhhh," I heard someone moan.

"Gogol?" I cried in spite of the danger.

"I've got him," said the man. "He's hurt. He needs help. Please, get in the boat. We have to hurry." I still didn't trust him, but he had Gogol. I had to stay by my friend.

"Okay, okay, I'm over here." I splashed my arms so he could find me.

"That's a good lad," the man said kindly as he hauled me into his boat. I wanted to be brave. Show him I was tough. Scare him a little so he wouldn't harm us. But I was doing that shaking and shivering dance again. My teeth were chattering so hard, I couldn't get any words out.

The man held up a glowing lamp and looked me over carefully. "Here, wrap yourself in this blanket." I did as I was told, then crept back to be by Gogol, who was slumped on the floor of the floater, still moaning. He didn't sound too good. And he had a red-stained rag pressed to his head.

"Will he be okay?" I asked between chatters.

"He has quite a serious cut to the head, I'm afraid. He needs medical attention immediately!" All the time the man was talking, he was pulling his two sticks with a strong, steady strokes.

We made it to the shore sooner than I thought we would. As we moved the floater out of the water, the man pointed to a horse-drawn two-wheeled transport tied up just ahead. "I've a wagon there. Help me move your friend."

"And if I won't?"

"There's no time to argue with you, boy. I'm taking

your friend where he can get some help. With or without you." Then he lifted Gogol and began to move toward the wagon.

"With me, then." I helped get Gogol settled in the back, climbed up onto the seat up front, and we set off for I-had-no-idea-where.

"Is it far?" I asked.

"Yes, how did you know?" the man said, sounding puzzled. "That's exactly where we're headed, the Farr town. We'll be there shortly."

"Why were you following us?" I asked as the horse pulled us along the darkened road. "And why are you helping us?"

"I wasn't, and is it so unusual for a stranger to offer help?"

"I don't know," I said. "You tell me. You're the Earthling here."

The man let out a very strange laugh. "Earthling?" he said.

"I mean . . . I was saying . . . er . . . the . . . ling . . . a . . . ling . . . a . . . ling. I seem to have a ringing in my ears. From being in the water, I guess. I can barely hear. Were you saying something?"

The man acted as if he hadn't heard me at all. He kept his eyes on the road, his shoulders hunched, and his mouth shut tight. After a while, he turned to me and asked, "So tell me, what were you and your friend doing out on the loch?"

"Fishing," I said.

"Fishing at night?"

"Umm . . . sure. Jackie says that's the best time to catch . . ."

"The monster, right?" the man interrupted. "Tell the truth. You were looking for the monster."

"We weren't looking for it, but we sure found it. Did you see it too?" I asked innocently.

"Yes, I saw it," answered the man. "But I beg of you not to tell anyone about it. The Loch Ness Monster is in danger. The more people hear about it, the more they'll want to capture it. Or worse." He sounded so sad, so serious, I decided to tell him the truth.

"Don't worry, we won't tell anyone. We don't really care about the monster," I said. "We were out there looking for a lost friend."

"In the middle of the loch? In pitch dark? On a cold, foggy night? How do you expect me to believe that?"

"Because it's the truth," I said. "He's a member of the Rak clan, and . . ."

"Rak clan!" the man cried. "You're the second one to bring up the Rak clan, tonight. In fact," he said as he pulled the wagon to a stop in front of a small, low building, "I thought you looked familiar. Are you related to a certain Cornish and Kind-of-ish?"

"Arms and Xela!" I shrieked.

"What?"

"I mean, 'arn-a-goshin,' " I said. "It's an old family expression. Means 'oh my gosh.' Anyway, Cornish and Kind-of-ish are my cousins. How do you know them?"

"I played a round of golf with them and then we had dinner together."

"You wha—" I was speechless. Was I the only one who took a mission seriously? Searching for She-Rak, guarding the lake, and battling monsters, while all the while Arms and Xela were playing games and having a nice supper, and Gogol was off on his personal quest. *That does it*, I thought, *if they can all do their thing, I'm not leaving this planet until I learn how to make a call.*

23

Xela Zim Bareen

My jaw fell open; the blood drained from my face. My heart started to pound. I tried to speak, but all that came out was, "Eh, uh . . . iba . . . wha, um . . ."

"My thoughts exactly," Arms said. We both stood there staring at Baby Nessie, a creature that looked a lot like a tadpole with spiked hair, which could only mean one thing.

"SHE-RAK!" I finally managed to scream. I ran over and gave him a hug.

"Ugh?" She-Rak croaked, not at all sure what was happening.

Jackie looked at me. "What did you call Baby?"

"She-Rak," I answered. "That's his real name." I

turned back to face She-Rak. At least I think I was facing him. She-Rak has two eyes in the front but his head has markings all around it that look like eyes. From a distance, you can't tell which is which. "She-Rak! It's me, Xela!"

"I thought your name was Cornish," Jackie said.

"Right," said Arms. "Xela Cornish Zim Bareen Ness."

Jackie scratched his head. "Aye, if you say so. It's a fine name. But there's no point in talking to Nessie or her baby. They don't understand human language."

"Of course not," I said to Arms. "He needs a pan-tawky." I started to move towards She-Rak to hand him mine. She-Rak just backed up toward Nessie.

"Wait a minute," I said. "He doesn't recognize us because we've turned ourselves into humans. There's only one thing to do. Hand me some haggis, Arms."

"Arms?" Jackie said, sounding more and more confused. "I thought you said your name was Cavendish."

"Kind-of-ish," she answered as she plopped some haggis in my hand. "But they call me Arms because I have four . . . oops, I mean, *two* arms. See?" she asked, holding them over her head.

"Oh," was all Jackie could say.

"Arms, I'm going to use the haggis as bait so I can get close enough to She-Rak to give him my pan-tawky. That way you can talk to him, and Jackie can follow what's going on."

"Okay," she said as I held both out toward She-Rak. He looked confused but took them anyway. As he did, the human words slipped from meaningful to gibberish.

Jackie grabbed me by the sleeve and turned me around. He was talking. I had no idea what he was

110

saying, but I could see the questions on his face. I wanted to help him understand, but without the pan-tawky, I didn't know any Earthling languages.

"Ump datta sump ta chatta vump," I said in Pan-PUese. That threw him into total shock. He took several steps backward. His eyes locked on me, confused and scared. I just smiled and shrugged. It was all I could do.

Meanwhile, She-Rak was jumping up and down. Arms hugged him and started explaining what had happened. *Mission accomplished,* I thought. Now all we had to do was hook back up with the guys, dial the coordinates for home into the WAT-Man, and step into a wormhole. I smiled. She-Rak looked at me and smiled back. Then he looked up at Nessie. He was explaining something to Arms, but I couldn't tell what he was talking about. Arms looked amazed. She laughed and handed me her pan-tawky.

"Arms wants me to explain this to you, Xela," She-Rak said. "When I got to Earth, I slithered into the lake to try to find a snack."

"That figures," I said. "So?"

"So while I was feeding off the bottom, I met my friend here."

Jackie came and stood next to me again. He spoke as if he was in a trance. "Baby. You . . . can . . . talk."

"Only because I'm holding this, Jackie lad," he said, opening his chubby hand so Jackie could see the pan-tawky unit. The boy's gaze locked onto the silvery device. "Anyway," She-Rak continued, "this magnificent creature here is no monster. This is my Aunt Tik."

"What?" I shouted, jerking my head around to look at the so-called monster. "Your *aunt?*"

"Well, not my true aunt," She-Rak explained as he

111

waddled over to Nessie. "I just call her that. But she is a life form from my home planet."

"Home planet?" Jackie repeated, absently.

I shook my head. "Wait, you're telling us that the Loch Ness Monster *just happens* to be from planet Skarfenbarph? How did she get here?"

"Let her tell everyone," She-Rak said, touching the pan-tawky to the creature. I couldn't see any change, but I knew the linguistic force field now surrounded her.

The monster looked at me, blinked its eyes, and grinned. Jackie let out a gasp as the creature began to talk. "Allow me to introduce myself," she said. "I am Tik-Tak, also known as mission specialist number zero-four-eight-zero."

"You're a Goner!" I shrieked.

"Oooohh, so am I," Jackie moaned as his knees gave way, and he collapsed onto the floor.

24

Rubidoux

"Where are you taking him?" I cried as the man hauled Gogol inside the small building.

"To a hospital," the man said. "I told you he needed medical attention."

"Oh, yeah," I said in my most professional mission specialist tone of voice. But this stranger wasn't waiting to hear my opinion on the subject. He'd already flown up the steps with Gogol in his arms and was shouting out orders as I entered.

"Bandages. Needle. Thread. Hot water. Carbolic acid," he commanded. No one moved. They all seemed too stunned to obey. Finally, one young man, wearing a smock decorated with blood stains, managed to stammer, "Who, who . . . who . . ."

"Who Nose!" I shouted.

"Who are you?" he asked.

"I am Dr. Joseph Lister," the stranger said.

"Oh my gosh. Oh my golly," cried a woman helper. Then, almost as if a hitsu had chimed, everyone ran from the room.

"What's going on?" I asked Lister.

"Be patient."

"Me?" I said. "No way, I feel fine. Gogol's the patient!" The man glared at me, but before he could speak, people came running back in.

"Needles!" one yelled.

"Bandages!" said another.

"Saw!" a young man shouted, hold up a jagged tool.

"Saw?" Lister said. "The boy has a head wound; I don't think amputation will help him."

"Oops, sorry," said the embarrassed helper. He threw the saw on the floor.

"We have no time to waste," Lister said, "the boy's lost a lot of blood. We need to get him into the operating room right away." Everyone followed Lister's commands as if he were the Grand DOO-DUH or something.

"Hey, just who *are* you?" I asked.

"No time for that now," answered Lister. "Follow me. Your friend is going to need your help too."

Figures, I thought. Then Lister pushed Gogol into the operating room. And brought him back out just as fast. "A disgrace," he cried. "I can't operate in there. No one should." He turned to one of the women in the room. "Quickly, nurse. Every moment counts. Find a brush. Carbolic acid. Hot water. And start scrubbing everything down. This boy's life depends on it."

Just as the nurse left the room, a great tall man entered. He was covered in blood and guts and gore. It was under his fingernails and matted in his hair. "Wait just a moment here," he bellowed. "What's going on?"

"Dr. McClean," stammered the young guy. "Dr. Joseph Lister is here."

"I don't care if it's Hippocrates, himself. No one gives orders in my hospital, except me!"

"Look, Doctor," said Lister. "I know this is all rather sudden, but operating on this boy under these conditions could mean the end of him."

"How dare you? I am a surgeon and a pretty good barber as well," barked McClean. "I've operated on hundreds of people in that room." He pointed to his gross, gutsy apron, and went on. "I wear this apron with pride. Look at this blood. It bears witness to my many operations."

Not a pretty thought. Lister must have agreed because he just wouldn't back down. "I'm sure you are a brilliant surgeon, but how many have died afterward from infection?"

"Well, sir," McClean admitted, "it's true that I often must tell a family that though the operation was a success, the patient died. We lose at least half our patients after surgery. But that is true in all hospitals, not just mine."

"But it is unnecessary, Doctor," Lister said. "I've been able to prove on patient after patient that disinfecting yourself, your tools, and your operating room can save the vast majority of patients from dying while in your care."

"What a ridiculous notion," said McClean.

"Dr. McClean, sir," interjected the younger doctor, "Lister's right. I've read what he's done. It's a miracle, sir."

"Blind luck," McClean said. "Think about it. For what Lister says to be true, we'd have to believe that little germy things, smaller than the eye can see, hop off my hands or apron or knife, jump into the open wounds of my patients, and then grow and multiply, until they kill the patients with infection."

"Excellent!" said Lister. "You seem to actually have a grasp of the concept, doctor. Now all you need do is believe it." He pushed Gogol past the Blood and Guts guy and into the room that the nurses and young doctors had been scrubbing. "And whether it's blind luck or science, this is my patient. I will treat him as I see fit. Now everyone, out of the room!"

25

Gogol

"Uuuhhhh," I moaned. "Uuuuuhhhh." I wanted to scream, *Get me out of here. Don't let anyone touch me!* One look at the strip of Alzorian skin running down my back, and whoever this person was who was hovering over me would be yelling for the police. Where was Rubi? Why wasn't he here? I wanted to ask, but "Uuu- uhhh. Uuuuuhhhh," seemed to the only sound my mouth could form.

I had to admit groaning helped somewhat. I hurt a lot worse than when I caught an Earthling disease and spent what seemed like half a lifetime at the SWEET Shop on Roma. But feeling bad or not, I had to try to sit up. I had to get out of here! I managed to get an arm under me, then pushed myself up. "Ow!" I screamed.

"Quiet," said a man standing over me. "I'm a doctor. And if you'll only trust me, everything will be fine."

Easy for you to say, I thought. *You fit in here. No one will hurt you for being different. But me, I'm a mutant. An alien being!* I tried again to get away.

"None of that, young man. Just lie still, so I can see how deep your wound is." I have to admit, his voice was so calm and his touch so gentle, I wanted to do as he said. I could feel him cleaning the wound on the back of my head. Then he rolled my collar back and lifted my hair off my neck. He was very still. I knew he was inspecting my alien stripe. I waited for the scream.

But it never came. Much to my amazement, all he said was "Very interesting." *This is the end,* was all I could think. *What did he mean by "interesting"?* I'd been discovered, and there was nothing I could do. I felt dizzy and sick to my stomach. I could hardly move.

"I am going to sew up the wound on your head," the man said without emotion. "Sadly, I have no anesthesia, so you will feel some pain. I apologize in advance."

Pain, I thought. *Pain! What physical pain could compare to the pain of being discovered?* Why wasn't he saying anything? Why? . . . Why? My thoughts became cloudy; I was overwhelmed. I teetered on the edge of consciousness, then everything went black.

"Gogol. Gogol, wake up," I heard someone say. SMACK!

"Ow! Rubi, leave me alone," I moaned, then turned

118

over on the bed—except I wasn't in bed. I was in a chair, and Rubi and the man I had seen earlier were hovering over me.

"Gogol," said Rubi. "I'm sorry to hit you, but you must wake up. *It's important!*"

But I didn't want to wake up. I knew what was important. I was being hauled away. Thrown in jail. A prisoner on Earth. Rubi grabbed my shoulder and started shaking it. "Cut that out," I said as I tried to push him away.

"Gentle, son, gentle," Dr. Lister chided Rubi. "He's had a bad shock."

"Nothing compared to the one he's about to have," said Rubi. "And you said he had a really hard head. Which, of course, all his friends already knew."

"Not funny," I said, my eyes flying open.

"I knew a good insult would bring you around," said Rubi. Then he put his arm around the man. "Gogol, I'd like you to meet Dr. Joseph Lister, the one who saved your little Alzorian hide."

"Rubidoux!" I cried.

"You mean Hamish," said Rubi.

I looked over at Dr. Lister. "That's right. I meant Hamish Rubidoux. Part Scottish. Part French."

"And all Douxwhopian," said Lister. Even with my head aching and throbbing, I could feel my eyes grow big with surprise.

"You're a *Goner?*" I cried.

"From what Rubi has explained, I suppose I am. I *have* been gone from the P.U. for a very, very long time now. Once contact was broken, so many years ago now I can hardly remember, I figured Earth was my new

119

home. Then, quite recently, rather suspicious things began to happen.''

''Such as?'' I asked.

''Two look-alike boys named Cornish and Kind-of-ish searching for someone in the Rak clan.''

''Xela and Arms,'' said Rubi. ''The other half of our mission specialist team.''

''Then you,'' Lister said to Rubi, ''looking very much like the other two and calling out the name of Dr. Autonomou.''

''But why were you following us?'' I asked, sitting straight up in spite of the pain.

''I wasn't,'' said Lister.

''Come on,'' said Rubi. ''You stayed behind us stroke for stroke. We heard you.''

''You were in my usual spot,'' Lister said. ''I'm always there, every third Monday, middle of the night, just off the western shore.''

''Why?'' I asked.

''To visit my sister.''

''Huh?''

''My sister. My twin, actually. Some call her the Loch Ness Monster, but I know her as Tic-Tak. We came to Earth together as mission specialists, but for some reason her B.O. failed.''

''That's horrible,'' I said.

''She's made peace with it,'' said Lister. ''But she is very lonely. That's why I make it a point to visit her at least once a month.''

''But the monster tried to knock us over,'' I said.

''Nonsense, she's just a little playful. I'm sure she expected to see me when she came to the surface. The shock of finding you two probably made her a little careless in her rush to submerge.''

"I'll say.''

"I saw your Alzorian skin, Gogol, when I pulled you into my boat. That confirmed my suspicions about you and your friends.''

"So that's why you wouldn't let that so-called-doctor McClean near me.''

"That and the fact that the man was filthy, covered in blood and guts, and no doubt a better barber than a surgeon. You would have gotten an infection from the germs on him far more dangerous than the wound you came in with. Cleanliness, one of the most basic principles in the universe, could save millions of lives here,'' Lister said. "That is, once I can convince doctors of its value.''

"Dr. Lister,'' said Rubi as he threw his arm around the man, "I bet someday someone names a great scientific breakthrough after you. I can hear it now. Mister Lister. Clean Mister Lister. Mister Clean. Lister Clean. . . .''

"Spit it out, Rubi!'' I said.

"Lister-een!''

"Perfect,'' I said. The doctor had a wide grin. "Lister-een. Leaves a fresh, clean taste in your mouth, don't you think?''

26

Xela Zim Bareen

With Jackie lying still as a stone, She-Rak rushed to his side. "Make way, make way. I'm a doctor."

"She-Rak," Arms said. "Last I checked, you were a volunteer at the health center. Not a doctor."

"Right, and you're no mission specialist, Arms Akimbo," She-Rak said.

"Oops." She blushed. "Got me."

"Jackie! Can you hear me?" She-Rak shouted, cradling the boy's head with one hand and gently slapping him with the other. But Jackie was out. "Jackie!" he shouted again. Then She-Rak dipped his tail into the cold water and flicked it into Jackie's face. That did it.

"Aahhh!" Jackie shrieked.

"Not bad for a student," I said with a smile.

"Ooohh, where am I?" moaned Jackie.

"It's me, Jackie. The one you call Baby, remember?"

"Baby. But how . . . why . . ." Jackie muttered as he sat up and looked at us. A sense of determination seemed to come over him. He stood up, brushed himself off, and spoke in a firm voice. "Let's just everyone tell me what's going on here, shall we?" Then he seated himself on a rock. "We'll start with you, Baby, or whatever your name be."

"My name is She-Rak, and I know it must sound strange, but I'm from another world."

"So are we," I added.

Jackie looked at Arms and me and grinned. "You may be from another county, but it strains the imagination to believe they dress and sound like Scots on another world."

"No," I explained. "We changed ourselves to look like you when we first got here. You were the first sample we saw."

"Sample?"

"Right," Arms explained. "We patterned ourselves after you. That's why we all look so much alike." Jackie held up a shiny metal tray and stared into it. Arms looked over one of his shoulders, and I looked over the other. The three of us stared at our reflection. It was obvious we all had the same face.

Jackie threw the tray down with a clang. "Well, I wish you'd have chosen someone else," he said. "And what about you, Baby? If you're from another world, why don't you look like me, too?"

"I don't know the secret of B.O.," She-Rak admitted.

"Simple," Jackie sniffed. "Wash."

"Won't help with the B.O. we're talking about," said Arms. "Biological Osmosis is one of the most closely guarded secrets of our society."

"We know it," I said, pointing to Arms and me. "But She-Rak doesn't."

"I knew it, too," the Loch Ness Monster said. "But it didn't work."

"What do you mean?" I asked.

"When I came to Earth, I selected a life form to pattern myself after, but for some reason, my B.O. never worked."

"I had that problem on my last trip to Earth too," I said.

"The strange thing about my case," said Nessie, "was that my brother didn't have any problem. Only my B.O. stunk."

"Your brother?" Xela asked.

"My twin, actually. Dr. Autonomou agreed to send us to RU1:2 together."

"So what happened?" I asked.

Nessie sighed. "When my B.O. went bad, we tried to get me back to Roma, but no luck. Eventually, for reasons we've never understood, all communication was cut off. We were stranded. My only choice was to take up permanent residence in a place with a constant food supply. This lake is the deepest one in Scotland. Its bottom is pure slime. What better environment for a Bottom Feeder?"

"I'll say," said She-Rak licking some slime off his skin.

"And this brother of yours, who did he become?" I asked.

"Doctor Joseph Lister."

"Lister!" Arms shouted.

"You know my brother?" asked Nessie.

"Yep," said Arms. "Met him shooting at the little creatures. . . . Oops . . . I mean playing a game he called golf."

"He comes up here to visit me about once a month," said Nessie. "I get kind of lonely, you know."

"I come every day I can," said Jackie. Nessie turned to Jackie and gave him the saddest look imaginable.

"I know, but I've always feared that one day you'd grow up and come no more."

"Ah, Nessie," said Jackie, patting her on the neck.

"Well, fear not," interrupted Arms. "Your days living in the loch are over."

"What do you mean?"

"We came to Earth to find She-Rak and bring him home. But there's no reason we can't take you, too."

"Home?" Nessie asked.

"Sure," I said. "And your brother too, if he'd like."

Nessie got very quiet. "You can take me with you," she finally whispered. "I hadn't thought of that."

"Don't go," Jackie said in a low voice. "You're my friend, Nessie. My best friend. If you leave, what will I do?"

Nessie smiled and put her head right in front of Jackie so they could look eye to eye. "I know it won't be easy for you. And it won't be for me either. But you'll be okay, Jackie. I promise you will. You'll have lots of friends along the way. And I hope you'll always save a special place in your heart for me."

"I don't know if I can do that," Jackie said sadly. "My heart will be broken."

"Paging Doctor She-Rak!" Arms said. "Broken heart on floor one."

She-Rak waddled over to Jackie. "I don't think I can fix your broken heart, Jackie, but think about this. Your friend Nessie has been living like a prisoner under loch and key. She misses her home, her family, and her friends back on planet Skarfenbarph."

Jackie said nothing and turned away.

"It's time for her to go home," said She-Rak gently.

The boy turned around and faced Nessie. "Can you come visit sometimes?" he croaked.

"Sure, I'll show up now and then," Nessie said with a smile.

Jackie sighed. A big drop of water rolled down his cheek and plopped onto the floor. He sniffed and wiped his face with his hands. Then he bent down and picked up his bag-o-pipes. "Okay," he breathed. "At least let me play you a last song before you go. Is that all right?"

"Better than all right, Jackie," Nessie said.

"Perfect," I agreed.

Jackie blew into one end of the bag and it puffed up. Then slowly, he began playing a familiar tune.

"Old Lang Swine!" Arms shouted. Then, she began to sing. "Should old acquaintance be forgot and never brought to mind!"

I joined in with, "WHOMP-BAM-BALOO-BA A WHOMP-BAM-BOOM!"

Finally, Jackie stopped playing and set down his pipes. "I must be going," he said. "It's almost dawn."

"Almost dawn? We have to be going too!" I said.

Jackie shook our hands. "Good-bye, Cornish and Cavendish. It was fun meeting you."

126

"Good-bye, Jackie," Arms said. "Don't forget our song."

"I won't." Turning to She-Rak, he said, "Take care, Baby." Then he flung his arms around the Loch Ness Monster's neck. "Good-bye Nessie. I'm going to miss you most of all."

Nessie smiled. "Hey, I'll be back, Jackie. You'll see."

"How will I know?"

"You'll know," Nessie said. "Be good, now."

"I will," the boy whispered.

Finally Arms said, "We need to go find Rubi and Gogol."

"Right!" Nessie said, sliding into the water. "Come on, Arms and Xela. Jump in."

"What?" I asked.

"It's freezing cold!" Arms yelled.

"Come on," the monster insisted. "One of you grab hold of my neck and the other hold on to She-Rak."

"Ohhhh!" Arms and I screamed as we hit the water with a splash. "Yeooww!"

"Grab tight and hold your breath!" commanded Nessie.

"Hold my breath?" Arms asked. "Doesn't a breath need to be in your lungs to be effective? Why would you want to hold it in your hand? What good would that do? Glub . . . glub . . . glub . . ."

"Good-bye, everyone!" Jackie yelled as tiny rivers of water streamed down his cheeks. Then he ran along the sides of the cave as the four of us did one final turn around the room. Just as we dipped into the murky cold water, I heard Jackie cry out, "I love you, Nessie."

Rubidoux

"Ouch!" Gogol cried as Lister's wagon took another hard bump. "My head is splitting!"

"Do you need me to tighten that thing up, Gogol?" I said, turning around to face him. I almost laughed out loud. The white cotton bandage wrapped around his head had slipped down to cover his eyes. He lifted it up and glared at me.

"No thanks, Rubi," he moaned. "How much farther to the lake?"

"Almost there," Lister said.

"So, Dr. Lister," I said, as the wagon took another bump in the road.

"Call me by my real name," Lister said. "Tok-Tak."

"Okay, Tok. I was just wondering if you've thought about what you'll do when you return home to planet Skarfenbarph?"

"That I have," he said. "I've been thinking about introducing my fellow Bottom Feeders to the game of golf. The only problem is, I'll have to find a way to make the balls taste bad."

"Taste bad?" Gogol asked, leaning up between us. "Is that so the Bottom Feeders won't mistake them for food?"

"No, that's to make them more appetizing," Tok-Tak said. "Bottom Feeders won't even think about playing a game unless there's food involved."

The early morning sun was just starting to come out as we got back to the lake. The fog, which had been so threatening last night, looked peaceful now as it lifted off of the lake in lazy swirls.

"Where are Arms and Xela?" Gogol asked. "I thought for sure they'd be back here by now."

"And well they should be," Lister said as we all climbed out of the wagon. "I happen to know they left dinner last night intending to come find you."

"You happen to know?"

"I followed them down the road for a bit, but they ran off when they heard my footsteps behind them."

"*They* heard you following them too?" Gogol asked. "Lucky for me you're a better surgeon than a spy."

"I'd say that's true, lad." Lister smiled.

"Oh, yuck," Gogol said. He was holding the WAT-Man upside down. Water was pouring out of it. "This thing was in my pocket. I hope it still works."

"What's the difference? We're not going anywhere until we find Arms and Xela, anyway," I said.

"Then we better get to it," Lister said. "We'll begin by searching the road to Inverness. They may have taken a wrong turn somewhe—"

"Look!" Gogol screamed, pointing at the lake. I jerked my head around in time to see something moving toward us just below the surface of the water. As the three of us stood there staring, Arms and Xela rose up out of the water and started waving their arms.

"Hello, Rubi!" Xela yelled.

"Hi, Gogol! Hey, Dr. Lister!" Arms screamed. They rose higher and higher out of the water until we could see they were riding on the backs of . . .

"Sister Tic!" Dr. Lister cried.

"She-Rak!" Gogol shouted.

"They must have found the key to the lock!" I said to Lister and Gogol.

"That they did," Lister said wistfully. The four life forms swam right up to us and staggered onto the shore.

"Group hug!" Arms called as we all moved in for a laughing, gasping, soggy reunion.

"Mission accomplished," Xela said. "Let's go home."

Gogol activated the WAT-Man. It hummed and crackled and sparked. "Everything looks ready," he said. "We'll be back on planetoid Roma in just a few moments."

Suddenly, Dr. Lister took a step back. "As tempting as that sounds, I feel I must decline," he said.

"What are you talking about?" I said. "This is your ride home, and . . ."

"I know, and I appreciate it, Rubi. But if I disappear now, it will delay the acceptance of my ideas by years.

Hundreds, maybe thousands of people will die unnecessarily. I can't walk away from that responsibility."

Everyone was quiet for a moment. Then Lister's sister Nessie spoke. "I won't leave you here alone," she said sadly. "I'll stay too."

"No, Tic, I insist you go," Lister said, reaching out and touching her. "You have suffered here as a monster long enough. It's time for you to go home."

A giant tear fell from Nessie's eye. "All right, brother," she said.

"Don't worry. I'll join you back on Skarfenbarph soon," Lister said.

"Don't count on it," I said. Lister looked surprised.

"Rubi's right," Gogol said. "The Grand DOO-DUH said this would be the last rescue mission to Earth."

"Forever," Arms added.

"Give the DOO-DUH a message for me," Lister said. "Tell him they can't give up on us a second time. If he makes you stop, our fate is on his hands. He must find a way to keep the missions going."

"I'll tell him," Gogol said, as he entered the coordinates and summoned the wormhole. A cold wind began to whip around the six of us.

"Roma-rama!" Arms shouted.

Lister smiled and waved. "I'll be home as soon as I can get my golf score below eighty!"

"Go get 'em tiger," I said as we vanished into the intergalactic void.

28

Arms Akimbo

The floor of the lab felt cold, hard, and wonderful as I tumbled out of the wormhole. Quick as I could, I B.O.'d into my regular old four-armed self. As I felt my DN-Aydoh changing back, I heard Autonomou's voice scream out.

"What's the matter, Doctor?" I asked, once my B.O. was perfect. "Aren't you glad to see us?"

"Of course I am, Arms!" she yelled from the computer control panel. "But I'm afraid we have a problem. Something huge has hitched a ride with you."

"What do you mean?" Gogol asked.

"The wormhole must have veered too close to another world and picked up a straggler," the doctor ex-

132

plained. "I'm trying to filter it out, but the file is so massive that . . ."

"No, Doctor! Stop!" screamed Xela.

"I can't stop it!" Dr. A yelled. "Here it comes!" The air in the lab throbbed as the wormhole opened for one more instant. We all rushed away from the center of the room to avoid being crushed as Tic-Tak, formerly known as the Loch Ness Monster, appeared before us.

"What's this?" cried Dandoo the DOO-DUH, standing next to Autonomou. They both backed up to the computer screen wall. "It's gigantic!"

Tic-Tak ducked her head and curled her tail in close around her body. She blinked her big eyes, brought her face right up to Autonomou, and smiled. "Hello," she cooed.

"Look, you," Autonomou fumed, "you have no business here! I demand . . ."

"It's okay, Dr. Autonomou," I said, working my way around Tic-Tak's massive body. "Don't you recognize her? It's Tic-Tak!"

"Tic-Tak?" Autonomou said distantly. Then her eyes lit up, and a smile crossed her face. "Tic-Tak! Ha, ha! It *is* Tic-Tak! Yahoo!" she boomed, jumping up and down.

"Looky, looky. I'm back, too, doctor," She-Rak proudly announced as he wiggled his way out from under Tic-Tak's tail.

"So you are." Autonomou beamed. "Excellent work, students. Wouldn't you agree, Dandoo?"

The grand-guy looked at us very seriously. "Yes, of course. I'm glad it all turned out well."

133

"But wait, Tic-Tak," Autonomou said. "Where's your brother, Tok?"

"It wasn't Tok-Tak's time," Tic explained. "He stayed behind to continue his mission. But he sent a message for the Grand DOO-DUH."

"A message for me?" Dandoo asked, surprised.

"Yes," Gogol answered, stepping forward. I could see him draw a deep breath as he tried to get his thoughts in order. "It's about future missions, sir."

"What future missions?" Dandoo scoffed. "I have already told you there will be no more missions."

"Yes sir, but . . ."

"Excuse me, but could I have a word with the DOO-DUH, please?" She-Rak asked as he slid between them. Gogol just glared. "Thank you," he continued. "Professor Toesis warned me about this bunch, sir." Autonomou and Dandoo looked at each other.

"She-Rak," I begged. "Please don't. . . ." But he went on.

"And now I see he was right," She-Rak said. I couldn't believe he was turning against us. "They have broken every rule. Challenged the High Council's authority. Put the peace of the entire Union at risk." Everyone was quiet. Dandoo had a smug look. Gogol was crushed. Then She-Rak added, "And I admire them for it."

"Huh?" I said.

"What are you trying to say, Mr. Rak?" the DOO-DUH asked.

"Just that everything they did was for a good reason," he answered. "Now that I've been to Earth, I can tell you it's not such a bad place. The High Council has made a terrible mistake. They should have never given up on it. And they should never have deserted those mission specialists.''

"All right, She-Rak!'' I squealed.

"The Bottom Feeder is right, Dandoo,'' Autonomou said gently. "We both know it. We can't turn back, now. The rescue missions to RU1:2 must continue. It is our duty.''

We were all in shock. No one had expected She-Rak to stand up for us like that. The Grand DOO-DUH looked thoughtful. He looked each of us in the eyes. Finally, he spoke. "Well,'' he sighed. "We'll see.''

"Yippee!'' I cried. We all surrounded She-Rak, patting him on the back and thanking him. Especially Gogol.

"Thanks for sticking up for us,'' he said.

"You're welcome. So, everyone, are we friends now?'' She-Rak asked hopefully.

I smiled. "Sure we are, baggy. Just don't splatter any more digestive juices on me, okay?''

"No problem,'' She-Rak laughed. Then he looked serious. "Hey, speaking of which,'' he sniffed the air, "what's that smell?''

"I smell it, too,'' Tic-Tak said.

"Please, Tic,'' Autonomou pleaded. "You're drooling on me.''

"Oh, sorry.''

"Oops!'' I said, reaching into my pocket. "I totally forgot. I brought you something.''

"A gift? For me?'' She-Rak beamed.

"Sort of a souvenir of our trip,'' I said, unwrapping the thing and holding it up. "Haggis!''

"Eeoowww!'' everyone groaned.

She-Rak looked at me and got all misty. "Thank you,

Arms," he said as he stuffed it in his mouth. "This means more to me than you'll ever know."

"I was afraid of that." I sighed as She-Rak chewed up the haggis, then pulled it out of his mouth and began to rub it on his skin.

What Are the Real Facts?

Goners is a work of fiction, but we've borrowed a lot from history:

Joseph Lister was an English surgeon obsessed with the idea of preventing the huge amount of deaths he saw happen each year in hospitals. Inspired by the discoveries of the French scientist, Louis Pasteur (naturally another Goner), he and his wife teamed up to prove that little things as simple as washing one's hands and sterilizing operating rooms and surgical tools could prevent germs from getting into open wounds and becoming infected.

Surgery in the 1860s was definitely not a picnic. Imagine, you are on the operating table and there is no such thing as anesthesia (chemicals that put you to sleep while you are operated on so you feel no pain). The surgeon's main duty was to operate fast, before the pain sent you into shock. The faster a surgeon could work the more highly they were regarded. Surgeons proudly wore aprons covered with blood, guts, and gore to prove they'd done many, many operations and were, therefore, at the top of their field. (Many also made money on the side as barbers.) When anesthesia was finally invented in the mid-1800s, surgeons like Lister saw that an opportunity existed to operate more slowly and carefully. But that would only work if infection could be prevented as well. Funny as it sounds, it took Lister years and years and years to convince doctors he was onto something. Most of them just saw him as some kind of nut.

Opportunity knocks. While most people laughed at Lister and his ideas, an American named Joseph Lawrence was so inspired, he went back to his lab and invented an antibacterial liquid he named after Joseph Lister—Listerine.

Another twosome impressed by the good doctor were the brothers Johnson and Johnson. Using Lister's ideas, they started a company that made sterile cotton to use as bandages. They were so successful, they went on to make baby powder and lots of other stuff you probably know about.

The Loch Ness Monster has been a part of the stories and folklore of the Scottish Highlands since the 500s when a traveling priest first claimed to have seen it. Many believe that if there is a "monster" it is the last of a type of dinosaur called a plesiosaur making its home in the deep, dark, murky water of Loch Ness.

Think the Kids from DUH
Are the Coolest in the Galaxy?
Read More About Them in
GONERS #7: SPELL BOUND

Rubidoux

"You know what I think," I said to no one in particular. "I think it's a waste of time sitting around like this. Waiting. Worrying."

"You can go back up to the surface, if you like," Autonomou offered. "I'll let you know as soon as we hear anything."

"I have a better idea," I said, looking at the images on the "Still Missing" side of the wall.

"Rubi, are you thinking what I'm thinking?" asked Arms.

"Wait a second," I said, putting my telepathic powers to the test. The purple tentacles on my head squirmed as I tapped into Arms's thoughts. "Yep! Exactly."

"No fair, you two," said Xela. "What is it?"

Arms smiled. "Rubi and I think we may as well go to Earth one more time."

"Impossible!" Autonomou barked. "Ridiculous! Irresponsible!"

"It would be better than just standing around waiting," I said.

"NO! I forbid it! Absolutely not!"

"Right, and if Gogol is guilty it's possible that the High C will find out about the lab and shut us down," Arms said, talking really fast. "So we should go get at least one more specialist back while we have the chance."

Autonomou turned away and mumbled. "Hmmm . . . logical. Good point."

"I have to agree," Xela added. "If there is a chance we can still save even one more Goner, then we've got to try."

Autonomou sighed. "Why not?"

"Roma-rama!" Arms yelled. "So who will we go after?"

"Well, we might as well start at the beginning. I'm pulling up the data on the very first mission specialist I sent to Earth."

The giant screen crackled to life and displayed the information:

MISSION SPECIALIST: #xxx
NAME: which?
HOME PLANET: Tina
SPECIALTY: unknown
EARTH TIME COORDINATE: 1690s

142

EARTH LOCATION: English Colony of Massachusetts
DESTINATION COORDINATES: EVL-BRU4U

"Geez, that's not much to go on," noted Arms.

"Harumph," Autonomou snorted. "We're lucky to have this much. When the High Council destroyed the connection to Earth, they also ordered the database erased, and . . ."

"We know, Doctor," Xela said gently. "You did the best you could in rebuilding it from memory. You did a fabulous job."

"Sure, we can take it from here," I said. "We've got the year, the location, and coordinates. Let's go!"

"I'll stay with Dr. Autonomou this time," Xela volunteered.

"Are you sure?"

"Yes. Besides I'm too worried about Gogol to be of any use on a mission."

Suddenly, Autonomou screamed, "Drag-nabbity!"

"What's wrong, Doctor?" I yelled.

"Ugh. It's this old equipment again. It will be the death of me. I have a solid lock on the entrance to the wormhole, but the exit on the Earth end isn't stabilizing. It's drifting in lazy circles."

"What does that mean?" Arms wanted to know.

"It means that if you went into the wormhole now, there's no telling where on Earth you would come out."

"So we have to wait?" I said impatiently.

"I'm afraid so," mumbled Autonomou. "Could take a long . . . WAIT!"

"I am already!"

"No, I mean, GO! Everything just fell into place. Go now while you have the chance!"

"Arms, grab two pan-tawky language translators," I said as I moved to the center of the room.

"I've got them," Arms said as she came and stood beside me.

"Rubi, did you enter the coordinates into the Warp-Time Manipulator?" asked Autonomou.

"The WAT-Man is ready. All set, Doctor!"

"Excellent!" the doctor replied. "Xela, Universal maxsis crom-dimmer?"

Xela looked over the controls and flicked a clicker. "On!"

"Rayn-forest control sim?"

Flick, click. "Aligned. And the Think-U-Bators are on-line. We're ready."

"Coordinates for Planet RU1:2 confirmed," announced the computer.

"Wormhole materializing!"

Ice cold wind began to swirl around the lab. Arms and I joined hands. The chill that swept over me made me smile. The air pulsed and invisible waves of energy rippled through the room as an intergalactic highway opened before us. Arms and I joined hands, and stepped in.

"Good luck!" yelled Xela.

"This one's for Gogol," added Autonomou as we disappeared out of the lab.

They're super-smart, they're super-cool, and they're *aliens!*
Their job on our planet? To try and resuce the...

RU1:2
79729-1/$3.99 US/$4.99 Can

One day, Xela, Arms Akimbo, Rubidoux, and Gogol discover a wormhole leading to Planet RU1:2 (better known to its inhabitants as "Earth") where long ago, all 175 members of a secret diplomatic mission disappeared. The mission specialists scattered through time all over the planet. They're Goners—and it's up to four galactic travelers to find them.

THE HUNT IS ON
79730-5/$3.99 US/$4.99 Can

The space travelers have located a Goner. He lives in Virginia in 1775 and goes by the name "Thomas Jefferson." Can they convince the revolutionary Goner to return to their home planet with them?

ALL HANDS ON DECK
79732-1/$3.99 US/$4.99 Can

In a port of the Canary Islands in 1492, the space travelers find themselves aboard something called the *Santa Maria,* with Arms pressed into service as a cabin boy.

SPITTING IMAGE
79733-X/$3.99 US/$4.99 Can

THINGS CAN'T GET ANY EERIER ...OR CAN THEY?

Don't miss a single book!

#1: Return to Foreverware
by Mike Ford
79774-7/$.99 US/$.99 Can

#2: Bureau of Lost
by John Peel
79775-5/$3.99 US/$4.99 Can

#3: The Eerie Triangle
by Mike Ford
79776-3/$3.99 US/$4.99 Can

#4: Simon and Marshall's Excellent Adventure
by John Peel
79777-1/$3.99 US/$4.99 Can

#5: Have Yourself an Eerie Little Christmas
by Mike Ford
79781-X/$3.99 US/$4.99 Can

#6: Fountain of Weird
by Sherry Shahan
79782-8/$3.99 US/$4.99 Can

#7: Attack of the Two-Ton Tomatoes
by Mike Ford
79783-6/$3.99 US/$4.99 Can

#8: Who Framed Alice Prophet?
by Mike Ford
79784-4/$3.99 US/$4.99 Can

#9: Bring Me a Dream
by Robert James
79785-2/$3.99 US/$4.99 Can

#10: Finger-Lickin' Strange
by Jim DeFelice
79786-0/$3.99 US/$4.99 Can

#11: The Dollhouse That Time Forgot
by Mike Ford
79787-9/$3.99 US/$4.99 Can

#12: They Say...
by Mike Ford
79788-7/$3.99 US/$4.99 Can

#13: Switching Channels
by Mike Ford
80103-5/$4.50 US/$5.99 Can

Join in All the Daring
Environmental Adventure with

by Susan Saunders

Parsons Point lighthouse on the Atlantic coast, home to cousins Dana and Tyler Chapin, is part of Project Neptune, a nonprofit operation that works with sick and injured sea animals.

DANGER ON CRAB ISLAND
79488-8/$3.99 US/$4.99 Can

DISASTER AT PARSONS POINT
79489-6/$3.99 US/$4.99 Can

THE DOLPHIN TRAP
79490-X/$3.99 US/$4.99 Can

STRANDING ON CEDAR POINT
79492-6/$3.99 US/$4.99 Can

WITH
LYNNE REID BANKS

THE INDIAN IN THE CUPBOARD
60012-9/$4.99 US/$6.50 Can

THE RETURN OF THE INDIAN
70284-3/$4.99 US

THE SECRET OF THE INDIAN
71040-4/$4.99 US

THE MYSTERY OF THE CUPBOARD
72013-2/$4.99 US/$6.50 Can

And now in Hardcover

THE KEY TO THE INDIAN
97717-6/$16.00 US/$20.00 Can